Wizards War

Alderbrian Press

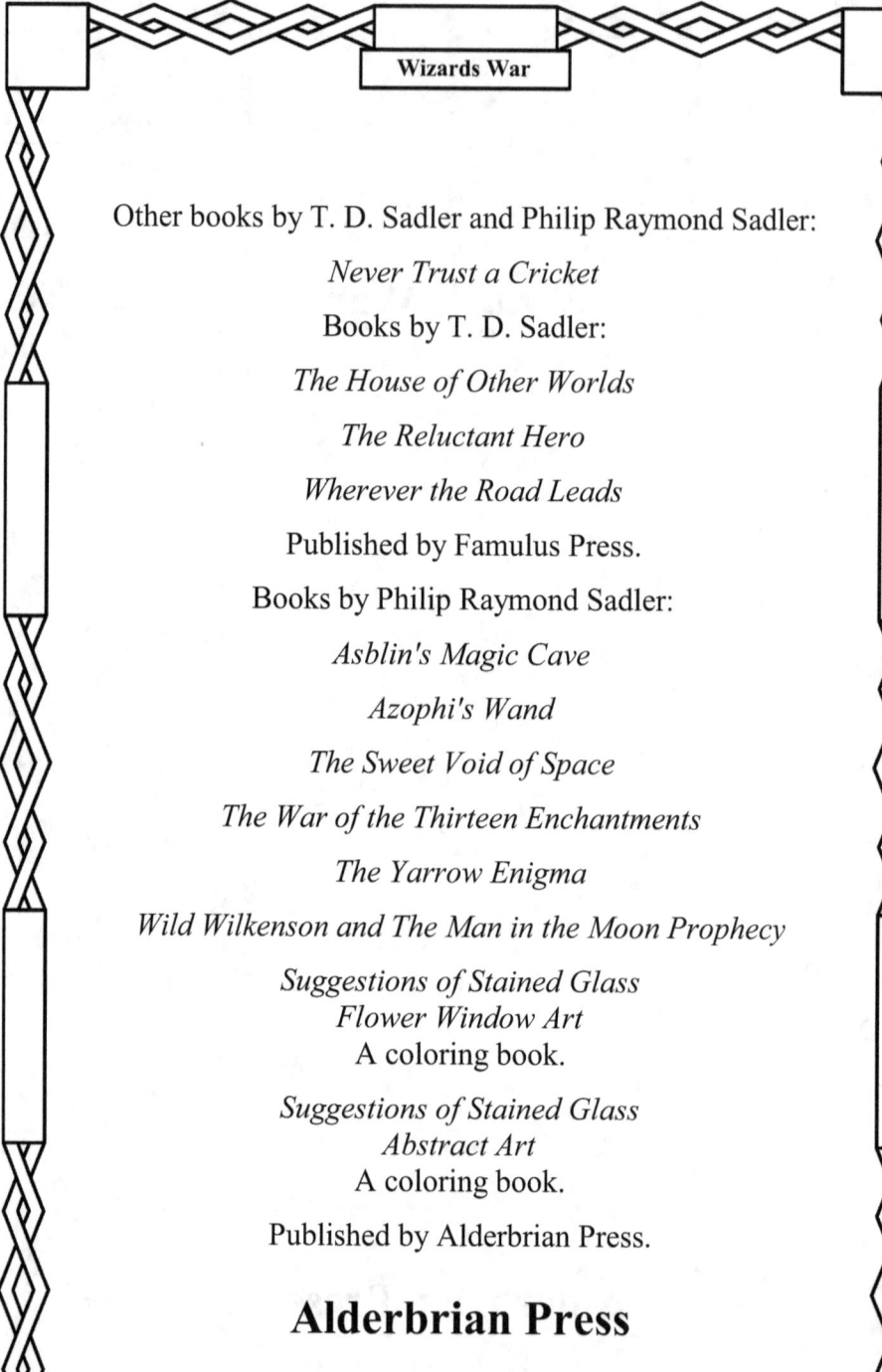

Other books by T. D. Sadler and Philip Raymond Sadler:

Never Trust a Cricket

Books by T. D. Sadler:

The House of Other Worlds

The Reluctant Hero

Wherever the Road Leads

Published by Famulus Press.

Books by Philip Raymond Sadler:

Asblin's Magic Cave

Azophi's Wand

The Sweet Void of Space

The War of the Thirteen Enchantments

The Yarrow Enigma

Wild Wilkenson and The Man in the Moon Prophecy

Suggestions of Stained Glass
Flower Window Art
A coloring book.

Suggestions of Stained Glass
Abstract Art
A coloring book.

Published by Alderbrian Press.

Alderbrian Press

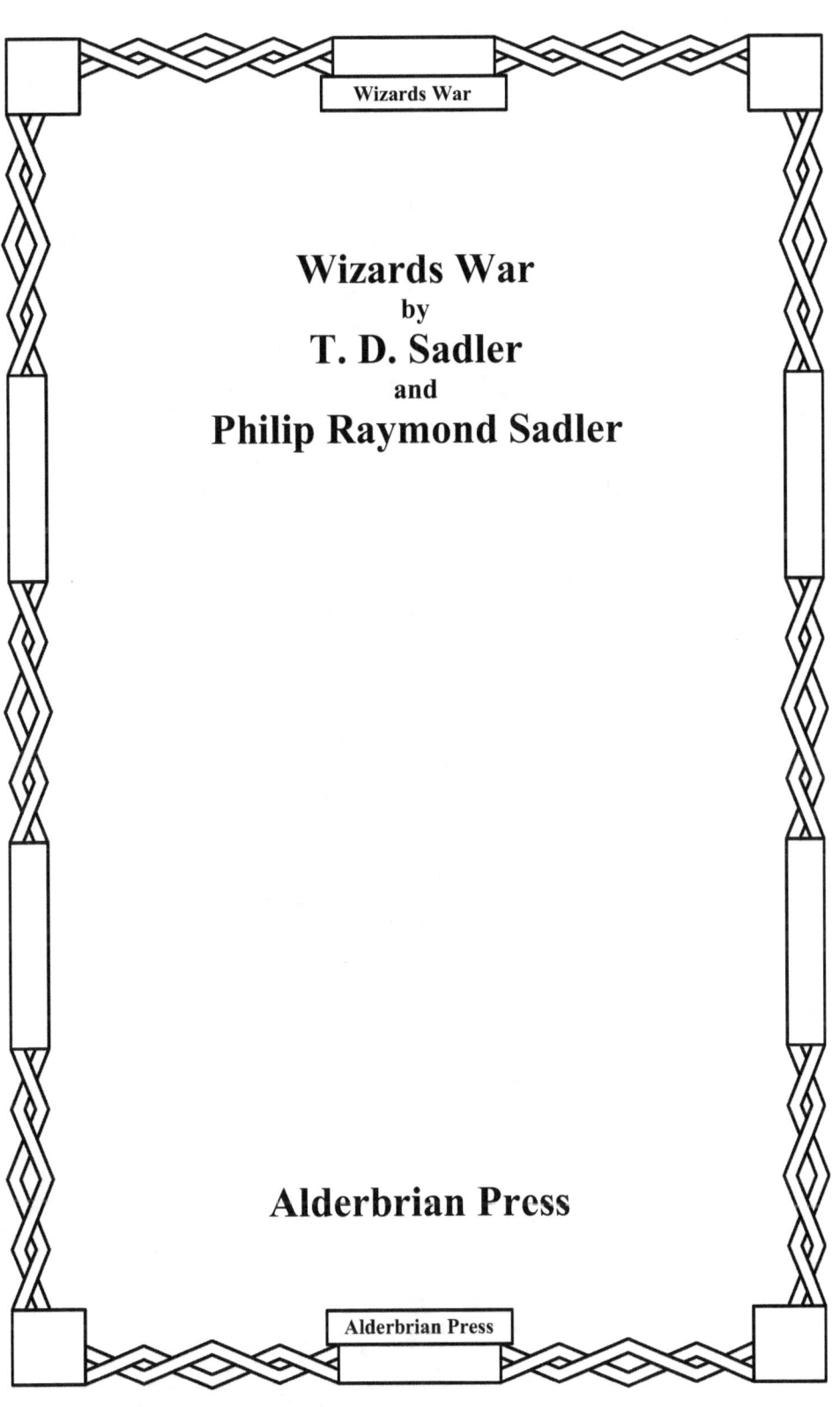

Wizards War
by
T. D. Sadler
and
Philip Raymond Sadler

Alderbrian Press

Alderbrian Press

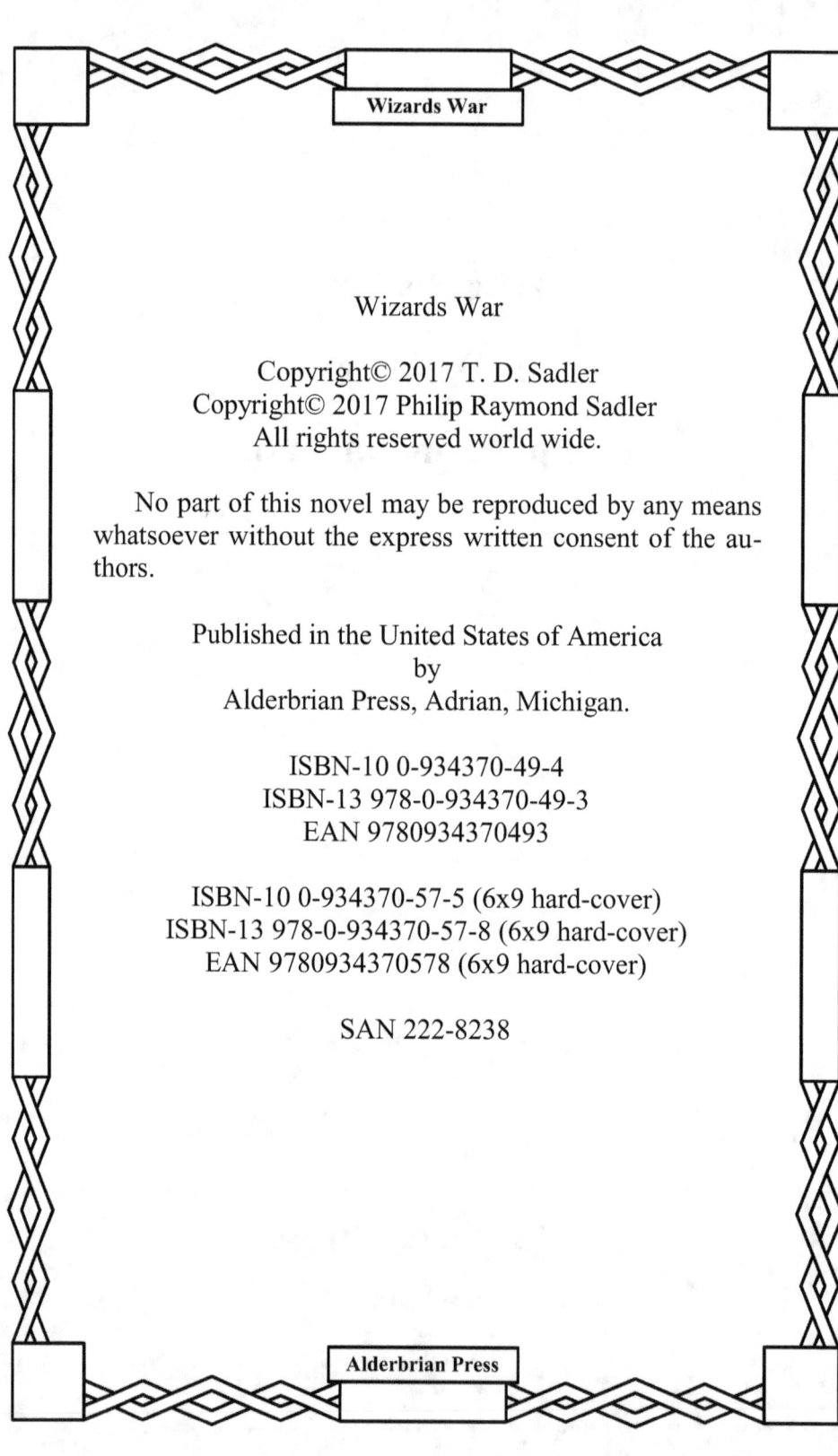

Wizards War

Published in the United States of America
by
Alderbrian Press, Adrian, Michigan.

ISBN-10 0-934370-49-4
ISBN-13 978-0-934370-49-3
EAN 9780934370493

ISBN-10 0-934370-57-5 (6x9 hard-cover)
ISBN-13 978-0-934370-57-8 (6x9 hard-cover)
EAN 9780934370578 (6x9 hard-cover)

SAN 222-8238

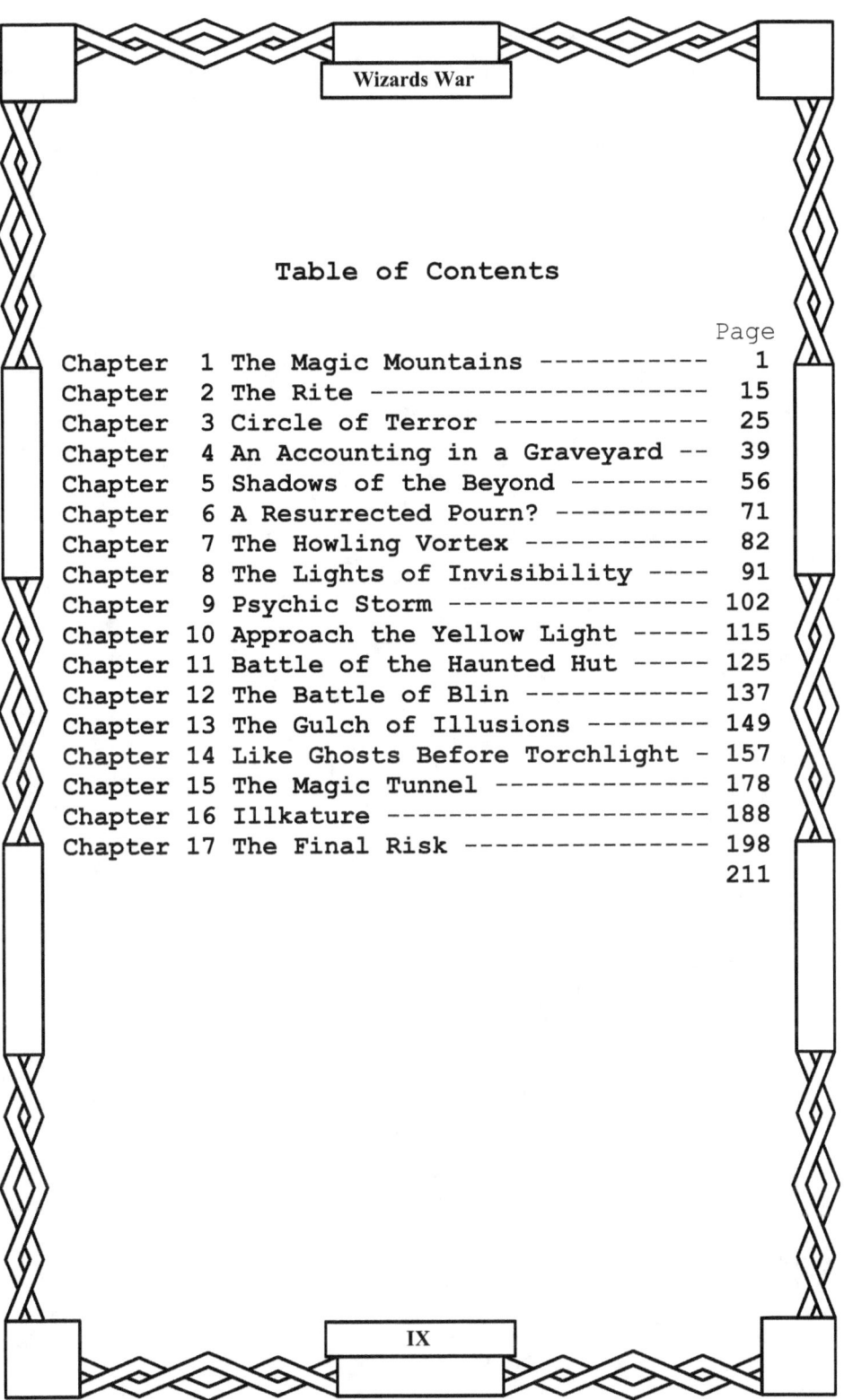

Table of Contents

Geography

Langdom, with its shining Capital in the North, is a temperate planet with one huge ocean and a single great land mass nourished by several rivers and fresh water lakes.

On the East and West coasts, lie deserts. On the North coast, lie the Near Wastelands, then a large tract of forests and fertile plains and hills. In the center, lie the Harlan Wastes and two leviathan mountain ranges separated by the Membling Pass. On the South coast, lie a large tract of forests and fertile plains and hills, and the Far Wastelands.

Well-traveled dirt roads connect the towns which speckle the habitable parts of Langdom.

Due to an ancient plague, and an almost forgotten Psychic War, the population of Langdom is small, and most dwell near the lakes and rivers. They occupy themselves with farming, hunting, and the crafts necessary for building and maintaining homes, farms and towns of an American Frontier type. Guns and gunpowder have not been invented.

The events herein chronicled occur upon the South end of Langdom.

Chapter 1

The Magic Mountains

The Wizard Monglom christened his forbidding citadel, Illkature, which, in the ancient tongue, meant, impenetrable fortress. It crouched across the Membling Pass like a black, glowering, nightmare beast. Its architecture was sharp and square; its buildings composed of huge, smooth slabs of solid magical energy. High walls of interlocking magic blocks surrounded it. Black habited Riders provided security, inside and out, constantly prowling the catwalks, battlements and pathways. A dome of transparent, gray magic afforded additional protection. Sheer obsidian mountains stood to the left and right, cutting Langdom in half.

He sat on his ornate, ebony throne, on a high dais, in the audience room of his towering, somber palace. At the tips of the wrinkled fingers of his right hand, a glistening obsidian ball nested in a receptacle near the end of that arm rest of his throne. He used this Talk-Globe, to issue edicts, to his Slavers, throughout Langdom. His hair was short and white, his face skull-like, his eyes black. He was unnervingly tall, and wore a flowing ebony robe, and boots.

There was a coal-colored door in the wall to his right.

A long, horizontal, rectangular window was cut out of the wall to his left, and framed a panoramic view of the mountains beyond the gray dome.

A similar window, before him, showcased the bleakness of the Harlan Wastes, which seemed to press, with malevolence, against the dome.

A black metal door stood to the left of this window.

He mused about his lifeless enemy. To think he and Pourn had been friends! He sent his mind two centuries into the past.

He was an aristocrat from the oldest and most wealthy clan on Langdom.

Pourn belonged to a middle class family from some obscure merchant town in the South.

He was accustomed to power and authority; to receiving whatever he desired when he craved it. The many luxuries he took for granted, Pourn was without. Yet, Pourn was happier.

Some quirk of fate brought them to the same university. Strange that two men, so unlike, should have become friends. Originally, they studied Law. Later, they discovered their mutual interest in developing their innate psychic abilities.

They invaded the university library. To their dismay, most of the data in the books addressing this subject, was contradictory, repetitious, pedantic, symbolic or confusing.

The meager information gleaned from these thousands of tomes forced them to seek other sources.

Quite by accident, they heard of an almost mythical group of monks who had set themselves apart from mankind to study the powers of the mind, to achieve a higher state of consciousness, and to aid humanity with their psychic abilities.

He and Pourn set out to find this group. They hoped to become members, or at the least, disciples. Their search took them to places they never imagined existed.

They encountered the cult in a cluster of mountains that stood on a dusty plain.

Monglom smiled; more like a grimace of pain. Those peaks were now a small part of his magic barrier mountains. A fitting revenge for those sniveling fools!

That religious sect was long dead.

He had gleefully seen to that.

The monks were divided as to the correct method of achieving their goals. One group believed in developing psychic powers through meditation; the other, through mind energizing drugs.

Monglom chose the rare powders because they brought results more quickly. He was not bred to pa-tience.

Pourn selected the way of meditation. He feared the effects of the drugs; some of the monks claimed the power powders twisted the mind.

Monglom recalled another event, and rage, which even two centuries and the demise of his adversary, had not diminished, reddened his gaunt visage.

Pourn had founded Langdom's Central Unity of Elected Representatives which had overthrown Monglom's noble, aristocratic family.

Two hundred years ago, in skirmishes with Pourn, and his followers, Monglom vanquished a hundred lesser magicians and wizards, robbing them of their knowledge and magical abilities.

He became overly confident and, sadly, underestimated Pourn's prowess. Foolishly, he forced a face to face confrontation with the benevolent Magician.

He and Pourn battled, furiously, in eerie ways previously unknown to Mankind. Their magical power salvos devastated the area surrounding the mountains of the monks, for a one hundred mile radius, creating the Harlan Wastes. Harlan, in the ancient tongue, means, war-scarred.

Despite the hellish destruction they wrought, they did not fight long.

Pourn defeated and paralyzed him, with psychic force. As he waited on his knees for what he was certain would be a swift death, he realized that he had nearly been Pourn's equal.

Pourn's beliefs would not allow him to steal the life of another. He had assumed an eventual confrontation with the Wizard and had long ago conjured a special prison not far from where Illkature stood and the final battle occurred.

It had been cleverly devised; a magical section of space and time. To those who traversed the plain, the prison was invisible, except for a subtle blurring which was mistaken for an unusual atmospheric phenomenon.

Pourn had mentally opened a wall of the prison, levitated Monglom inside, sealed the breach, released him from the paralysis, and cruelly walked away to the comforts of civilization.

From within the prison, the landscape appeared very hazy, as if viewed through a misty window. The only sound Monglom heard was his voice when he chose to speak to damn Pourn's foul soul.

The automatic, self-perpetuating energy field supplied him with the elimination of his bodily wastes and all things necessary to sustain his life, except companionship and freedom.

One hundred of his dark Riders stood before him, in paralyzed, mocking ranks.

During his nightmarish century of entombment, Monglom meditated on increasing his psychic powers. He realized, with regret, that he was too dependent upon his magical powders to gain pure psychic abilities. The performance of his brain had been permanently altered so he could not function properly without the drugs. He maintained his mental equilibrium with the Powders of Magic in his pocket pouches. Only a few grains per year were required.

The irony? If he had postponed his confrontation with Pourn for ten more years, with the unlimited powders of the mines in the mountains of the monks, he could have surpassed the magical prowess of the holy Pourn.

His next recollection caused him to do something which would have terrified his Riders and his palace slaves. He laughed: a short, sharp, uncanny cackling.

The opportunity for deliverance came, and he seized it.

He recalled the ensuing events from the memories which he had withdrawn from the mind of the Would be Wizard.

Harkath attended the university from which Pourn and Monglom had graduated. He combed the same tomes on hoary, arcane, supernatural subjects, and retraced, as best he could, their journeys in search of secret knowledge.

Over forty years, he developed psychic abilities of a level he never expressed to his relatives or friends. He had no need to brag, or to share his grand goals with common folk, as he would soon become the greatest of all the Psychic Wizards!

If Harkath could determine the exact location of the magic prison, and if he could breach its energy walls, it was his hope that a few grains of Monglom's distilled powders would be with the Wizard's remains.

These, he would analyze with his skill as a master chemist, and he would replicate them from the discrete powders still sealed within Monglom's mines. With the proper scientific controls, unknown in Monglom's time, Harkath was sure he could isolate out the harmful, mind destroying, elements of the distillate, and gain pure, augmented psychic power, to which even the Mighty Pourn would respond as a weakling. He, not softhearted, Saint Pourn, and not foolish, dead Monglom, would command Langdom. Forever!

Inspired by these noble thoughts, Harkath led his pack horse into the Harlan Wastes.

He kept the hood of his purple habit tight around his handsome features to block out the cold.

The deeper he and his steed delved into that depressing, desolate region, the more the usually sedate animal balked, pulling him off his intended course.

He stopped to soothe the horse, then closed his eyes and meditated.

To their right, there was a subtle energy creating foreboding in both man and steed.

Startled, Harkath realized that his reluctant, but sensitive, pack horse had been dragging him from his goal.

He led the complaining animal straight toward this energy. When it dug in its hooves, tossed its head, and refused to proceed, he concluded they were standing before one wall of the prison.

He led the steed to his right. When it appeared less stressed, he assumed they had moved beyond that end of the wall. He deemed this to be a corner of the occult prison.

He drew a stake and axe from his saddlebags. When he bent to hammer the stake into the hard, grainy earth, he was almost overwhelmed with delight.

A small square of glinting black earth, which had been fused by tremendous magical heat, marked the spot.

He led his horse back along the wall until it appeared less stressed, denoting the far corner of the first wall of the magic prison, and found its gleaming marker.

From these corner positions, he used his keen senses to determine the far corners of the jail, and found their fused earth squares.

He realized that the glittering markers were the boundary controls Pourn had forged from the earth.

If he could destroy these, this would collapse the spell which maintained the energy prison.

He pounded the stake into the earth, tied the reigns of the pack horse to it, and turned to his task.

No matter how mightily he hacked against the first

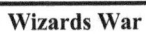

black, fused square, it suffered no damage.

He used the axe to dig away the earth surrounding the square, then the soil beneath it.

To his astonishment, the marker remained where it had been magically set, floating in air.

Though the square had nothing to support it, when he pulled upon it with all his might, it could not be moved.

He hacked at the ebony square again, but it did not even tremble.

He placed the long flat side of the head of the axe against the underside of the marker, used the handle as a lever against the edge of the pit, put his body weight into the matter, and still achieved nothing.

Failing these efforts, he returned the axe to his saddlebags.

He meditated, gathering his mental energy, held his hands toward the marker, and crackled orange lightning at the center of the block.

The earth, around and beneath the square, heated to red, and turned to glass, but the glinting marker did not grow warm.

Harkath, though frustrated and angry, felt respect for Pourn's ancient conjury.

He tried his final ploy.

He backed away from the invisible wall and placed both palms into where he felt the energy. He emanated his psychic might out of his hands, mingling it with the power of the prison.

Monglom returned to his own memories.

He keenly observed the trials and tribulations of the bungling Would be Wizard. When first imprisoned, he tried the very mergement in which Harkath was engaging, with no success, even with his vastly superior might. But, *this* was a momentous state of affairs. He swallowed the contents of one of his sacks of magic powder, pressed his palms to the barrier, beside Harkath's, and flooded his suddenly augmented energy into the force wall.

Monglom switched to the memories of the Would be Wizard.

Though he could see only the slight blur of the barrier, Harkath had an unexpected, terrifying feeling that his plan was going awry.

He tried to yank his hands from the wall, but they were stuck, as if they were held by someone on the inside.

His terror became horror.

It could be only Monglom!

Incomprehensibly, The Evil One had survived!

The combination of Monglom's powder-enhanced mind powers and Harkath's unique psychic energy vibrations overwhelmed the magic barrier at the spot of their mutual contact.

There was a strange rushing of air.

As Monglom drew Harkath into the psychic

prison, he propelled himself outside, into the glorious light of the sun.

Their shoulders brushed, as Monglom intended, and he sapped the Would be Wizard of his occult knowledge, memories and psychic abilities, leaving him bereft.

Monglom stepped away from the jail, and the wall repaired its breach.

Harkath screamed in despair and threw himself against the barrier. To release the monster Monglom upon Langdom had not been his intent! After opposition had been crushed, his own reign would have been benevolent! Monglom's rulership would be a horror to everyone! Harkath's beloved family would soon be enslaved! He raged and hammered his fists, uselessly, against the blurred energy shield.

These events serve me well, Monglom thought. Pourn's prison expects a living being to service. It has one. Pourn will not suspect I am free, and that he is in final, mortal jeopardy.

However, Pourn's prison did not recognize the poor Would be Wizard as Monglom. It assumed he was a Rider and placed him in suspended animation. His bruised fists remained pressed against the wall, but his sad, tortured mind was stilled.

Monglom turned off Harkath's memories and returned to his. He vacated the Harlan Wastes on the back of the pack horse.

During his unjust kidnapping, he had devised an energy screen to conceal his psychic signature from Saint Pourn, allowing himself the freedom to seek and destroy the vile Magician.

To that end, he once again ventured into the unhygienic infestation of civilization. His few surviving relatives and former servants had fearfully provided him with intelligence concerning Saint Pourn's whereabouts.

The goodly Magician, beloved of his foolish people, was performing healing in the plague-ridden, metal-mining hamlet of Audsburg.

Monglom traveled there by a carriage which had horses, but no driver. He paused among trees, on a high hill, which overlooked the outskirts of the dilapidated town.

He reached out with his clairvoyance.

Yes!

Yes!

There it was!

The unmistakable, sickening, sunny presence of Pourn!

He was alone in what appeared to be the town hall.

Monglom almost felt joy at these next recollections.

He stepped out of the coach and raised his hands over his head. He formed an orb of magic fire in his cupped palms, and hurled it forth.

The fireball increased in size until it was massive.

The town hall was enveloped in flames and reduced to cinders almost instantly, engendering an explosion which rocked the earth, shattering windows throughout the hamlet.

There were screams of surprise and panic from the townsfolk as they raced from their homes and businesses to see what had happened.

"Gather your loved ones and flee into the deepest caverns!" a wrinkled, stooped man cried out, in despair, from where he stood on the main street. He pointed his cane toward the hill and the black-robed, emaciated figure beside the gleaming, ebony coach. "The Evil One has slain the Great Protector Magician and is once again loose upon the land! As it was in my tragic past, so shall it soon be in my grievous present! I cannot bear the hellishness of it a second time!" He collapsed to his knees, sobbing.

Relatives, who did not have recollections of the Dark Times, ran to comfort him.

Monglom eagerly blanketed the village with his clairvoyance.

Yes!

Yes!

Neither a hint, nor a disguised semblance, of Pourn's vitality remained!

Not even the weak energy of his vanquished soul!

Final!

Fated!

Triumph!

Monglom shut off the flood of memories.

"All but the canny death blow I dealt the holy Pourn shall be obliterated from the history of my noble family," he told himself. "Now, I must return to the matters at hand."

Chapter 2

The Rite

The sun of early afternoon illuminated the emerald woods. Zones of shade and golden light fell across Halburd Road, which curved through the foliage like a huge, brown serpent.

One young tree stood closer to Halburd than the others. Its leaves were broad and smooth, its trunk, black, with a low crotch.

Mime, a dwarf, lay there asleep. His half-sleeved shirt, and his slacks, were blue; his boots, tan. His hair was brown and short; his face almost boyish. He was untanned, smooth of complexion, and clean shaven. He was, perhaps, thirty, well proportioned and firm, but not as muscular as one who works a farm. He was unarmed, which was unusual.

He often came to his meditation tree after he dismissed school. He enjoyed being lulled to sleep by the singing birds and the sighing wind.

He stirred, opened his blue eyes, leaned forward, under the drooping leaves, and concentrated on what had awakened him: the sound of many horses approaching, where the road curved out of sight.

The hoof beats grew louder.

Fifty mounted figures rode around the bend.

Mime caught his breath. It was not their number that surprised him, it was their manner of dress; jet black gloves, habits, sheathed swords and boots.

Their habits fluttered in the wind of their forward motion, but their hoods hid their heads and faces.

Mime noted white half moons on the backs of their gloves. Fear shook and chilled him. These were the Riders of Illkature; the devastating army of the despot Wizard Monglom!

The Riders looked unearthly as they rode through the alternating zones of golden light and black shade cast by the sun and the trees.

Mime could not believe a horrifying chapter of Langdom's history was being repeated. He grabbed a limb, swung out of the crotch, landed behind the tree, and dropped flat of his abdomen, in the relative security of the tall grass.

The Riders galloped past, swirling thick dust over the wide road. They thudded across the Old Haplan Dry Ditch Bridge, and disappeared around another bend. They were headed in the general direction of the farming community of Ullman, in the Valley of Pun.

Mime scrambled to his feet and raced across the bridge. He wondered how the Riders had escaped their Magic Prison. There was no way, unless —

He banished that horrifying thought, and ran faster. He would have to warn the people of Elpton, quickly, if they were to be saved.

He veered to his right, off the road. The dirt path he followed was nearly overgrown by the wild wheat that separated Halburd Road Woods from Elpton Woods.

***

The golden wild wheat thinned.

Elpton Woods rose from the horizon.

Mime paused between the trees. The heart of the woods had been hewn for the town. The red sun of late afternoon illuminated Elpton.

A large, white obelisk, dedicated to Pourn, stood on a black marble base in the center of the grassy square. The buildings had been developed around it.

The businesses were centrally located and the wide, dirt streets were sensibly situated.

The shops and homes were constructed of mud-and-straw bricks.

A ghostly silence hung over everything.

Mime ran out of the trees and down Main Street. He skidded to a stop just short of the first house.

Many hoof marks showed in the rough earth.

They were shaped like half moons!

The Riders of Illkature!

They had veered off Halburd Road and had invaded Elpton!

He raced from house, to shop, to house, to the school, where he mastered, but all were empty.

Broken doors and toppled furniture shouted of struggle.

He sat on the grass of the square and stared forlornly at the ground.

With a terrible sound, the obelisk behind Mime split in half, vertically, and the pieces fell to the lawn on his left and right.

Despair throbbed his heart.

His greatest fear was a *reality*!

Pourn was *dead*!

Pourn's legendary, imprisonment spell had somehow collapsed, allowing the Riders, and their evil master, to escape!

Mime's only consolation?

If History is being repeated, as it seems, the Riders are marching the townspeople to the mountains in The Harlan Wastes to slave in Monglom's secret Magic Powder Mines. A repeat of the fate of many of his ancestors.

Sly footsteps whispered in one of the bakeshops to the left of the forlorn obelisk.

Mime held his breath. He had just searched that shop and had seen no one!

A tall figure appeared in the shadows of the doorway. "What place is this?" a man said, with urgency.

"Elpton," the dwarf quavered.

"It is too *late!*" the stranger lamented. "If the enslaving Riders have penetrated *this* far, it is *too* late to warn *my* town!" He stepped out of the bakeshop. His hair was brown and short. His emerald eyes showed shrewdness. His rugged face was tanned almost to the color of his beard and mustache. He appeared to be in his thirties. His half-sleeved shirt and his slacks were green; his boots black. He held a large bow, with a nocked arrow. A full quiver was hung over his left shoulder. He bowed sadly. "I am Eeklan, of the town of Mislen," he said.

The dwarf stood up and returned the bow. "I am Mime, of the woods village of Elpton, which is no more," he said, dejectedly.

Eeklan placed the arrow into the quiver and slung his bow over his right shoulder.

He and the dwarf sat down on the grass.

"Your people have been captured, as have my own," Eeklan said, soberly.

Mime only nodded.

Eeklan leaned his head back at the pieces of the obelisk. "The Magician Pourn is dead," he said.

"I know," Mime lamented. "All is lost!"

"Some would believe so," Eeklan said. "I am not among them. There is hope. We are free. We can still fight. We will have friends inside Monglom's mine camps; they will fight."

"Monglom has potent Magic," Mime protested.

"Our Protector is *dead*. His Magic is no *more*!"

Eeklan grunted. "That *is* true," he admitted, "but we can still fight!" He stiffened. Something cold and hard was pressed against the middle of his spine.

"Remain still, or die!" a voice rasped.

Mime and Eeklan twisted their heads around.

A Rider towered behind them. Its face was concealed by the shadow of its hood and the early evening dullness. It grasped a sword in its gloved hand. The blade tip was against Eeklan's back.

Eight Riders appeared from between houses and shops. They had ten horses, one of which was a pack stallion. The faces of the Slavers were hidden by the shade of their hoods.

"Bind them!" the first Rider ordered.

Eeklan's bow and quiver were confiscated.

Two Riders drew ropes out of their saddlebags and bound the dwarf's and archer's hands behind their backs.

The first Rider sheathed its sword, caught its mount by the reins, and signaled for the party to follow.

They passed around the square, toward the one room schoolhouse. Its peaked roof was shingled with red clay squares, and its walls were constructed of mud-and-straw bricks. In the front yard, there were several wooden seesaws attached to a long metal framework.

The Riders tethered their horses to the seesaw rail and turned their hoods to their leader.

"Wait here," it said. It stalked down the dirt path, kicked the door open, and entered the dark school, its boots striking the floorboards noisily.

Mime flushed with anger, but said nothing. He and Eeklan tensely watched the doorway.

There were blue sparks from steel striking flint, then a steady yellow light. The Rider came to the doorway with an old oil lamp in its gloved hand. "Bring them in!" it ordered.

Mime and Eeklan were shoved roughly into the little school.

The Riders followed them closely.

There was a blackboard on the rear wall. Mime's stool, and his textbook-cluttered desk, stood below it. Many smaller desks and stools were lined up in rows in the center of the room. Each desk had books, slates and pieces of chalk on it. There were four large windows in the right wall and dusk was pressing somberly against them.

The lead Rider motioned to its companions.

They spread out and shoved the stools and desks aside, knocking books, chalk and slates onto the floor. The chalk, and some of the brittle slates, shattered.

Mime trembled with rage, but wisely remained silent.

Using some of the small desks, the Riders formed

a long table in the center of the floor. They placed nine stools around it and turned their hoods to their stern leader.

It placed the lamp on the floor, unbuckled its sword belt, and dropped the weapon at its boots. It untied the waist rope of its habit and allowed the garment to fall.

Mime and Eeklan gasped. The despised Riders of Illkature were more terrifying than history had recorded.

The skeleton's bones, which emitted a slight gray light, were held together by transparent magic that formed skin, flat black eyes, a brain, tendons, ligaments, muscles, a larynx, and lungs. There were no other organs, and no hint of gender. The only dark spots were its gloved hands and booted feet. It blinked its glow off and on, as though testing that ability, took up the lamp by its handle, and nodded to its macabre companions.

They removed their weapons and habits and the combined glow of their bones filled the school with grim, gray light. They gathered the coarse garments and weapons, and piled them onto the desks in one corner.

The leader Rider set the lamp in the middle of Mime's desk. "Sit on the floor and hold silence!" it commanded the prisoners. It parted its teeth in a hideous grin.

Mime and Eeklan complied. Mime's left shoulder was against Eeklan's right. Their backs were toward the door.

The leader skeleton sat on the stool at the far end of the line of desks so it was facing Mime and Eeklan. The other Riders took the first stools they came to.

The leader skeleton looked at a barrel-ribbed Rider on its right, and said, "Bwakk, how much time remains?"

Bwakk reached down, picked up a slate and a piece of chalk and began writing formulas. The other skeletons leaned close to follow the calculations.

***

"I will have us out of these ropes in no time," Eeklan whispered. "No twine made can hold old Eeklan, long."

Mime wrestled with his rough bonds and wiggled his hands free. He glanced at the skeletons, then moved his left hand behind Eeklan and began untying the archer's wrists.

"What magic did you use?" Eeklan whispered.

"Just common sense," Mime whispered. "Not bad, for a teacher."

"Is that what I have allied myself with?" Eeklan whispered. "Then, this is *your* school?"

Mime sadly nodded.

Eeklan felt his ropes drop away. He massaged his raw wrists behind his back.

***

Bwakk dropped the chalk onto the slate. "There are only *six* hours of Magic Life left for each of us," it reported, obviously agitated.

The leader Rider slammed a black gloved fist against a desk top. "It is as bad as we feared," it said. "There is not enough time for us to return to lord Monglom and have our lives renewed for these slaves.

"We should not have chased after those mounted prisoners when they escaped. They knew the territory, we did not. That is why we lost them.

"There are at least fifty miles between us and our main party, and they are herding their slaves toward Illkature. They have the Talk-Globe, so we cannot contact Monglom.

"It was blind luck that we stumbled across these two, and the solution to our quandary."

Bwakk turned its glow off, then on. "The Rite?" it said.

"By denying the largest of these slaves its life, we shall derive Life Time enough to reach Illkature, and we shall have the dwarf with which to purchase our Life Boost," the leader skeleton said. "The perfect solution. Prepare for the Rite!"

Chapter 3

Circle of Terror

The Riders began babbling, excitedly.

Eeklan whispered, urgently.

Mime nodded, eagerly.

The skeletons stood up and started around the end of the row of tables, toward the prisoners.

Mime and Eeklan leaped to their feet.

Mime spun on his heel and fled out the door.

Eeklan roared and hurled himself at the skeletons.

They toppled, left and right, like glowing dominoes.

Desks and stools were sent flying, in all directions.

The Riders cursed, in surprise and rage.

Mime ran to the seesaws. He untied the black pack horse, turned it around, and slapped it on one flank, sending it cantering toward the town square. He raced along the front wall of the school, turned left, and stopped. Breathing hard, he peeked around the corner, at the lighted entrance.

The angry skeletons charged out of the schoolhouse. They were bearing their swords, but they had

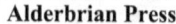
left their cumbersome habits behind.

The horses shied at the sight of them, but the Riders managed to mount. They galloped away, chasing the diminishing sounds of the pack horse's hoof beats.

Mime raced around the corner and into the school house.

Eeklan was bound, hand and foot, and lying face down, on what was left of the line of desks.

Mime freed him.

Eeklan rolled over, sat up, and swung his feet to the floor. He recovered his bow and quiver, and they exited the building.

Mime led Eeklan around the school.

They fled Elpton via a narrow, weed-grown dirt road which ran through the woods, straight North; toward Illkature.

***

The full white moon rose in the eastern sky.

The road dwindled to a path of grass.

The woods gave way to a wide, rolling grassland.

***

"Stop!" Eeklan said.

The moon and stars illuminated the territory.

Mime scanned the long grass. "What is it?" he said.

"Listen!" Eeklan said. He pointed left, toward a long semicircle of hills .

Mime held his breath. At first, he could detect

nothing, then he heard women and children scream-ing, or shouting enraged warnings for someone to stay away from them.

Eeklan strode along the inside of the line of hills.

Mime had to run to keep pace with the archer.

The semicircle ended on a flat expanse of grass. Two hills stood on opposite sides of the near end of a small valley; two more stood on opposite sides of the far end.

"In that Vale," Eeklan said. He darted across the field.

Mime made the same move a few seconds later. He was puffing.

They crept left around the first hill.

The screams of terror and rage were louder.

In the small valley, eight Riders ringed a group of women and children.

The people were unharmed, for the present.

The Slavers were walking slowly closer, decreasing the girth of their capture circle.

"We must help!" Mime said.

Eeklan rubbed his beard. "There is nothing you can use as a weapon," he said.

"An arrow?"

"No good," Eeklan said. "Their blades are longer. You could not touch them." He nocked an arrow.

Several horses wandered from the far side of the hill at the end of the vale. A Rider backed out of the slaving ring to soothe the mounts.

Eeklan re-quivered the arrow and darted across the level area of grass, to the far side of the second hill.

Mime followed as best he could.

The horse tending skeleton had gathered the reins in its right gloved hand and was watching its comrades closing the circle. Another minute, and the wrist ropes would be required. It raised its left gloved hand to one of the saddlebags on a gray horse.

Eeklan leaned around the small hill, stuck his bow out, dropped it around the Rider's neck, and jerked the skeleton backwards to the grass. Before it could cry alarm, he stamped the Rider's throat, then crushed its skull with his boot heel, causing its glowing, gelatinous brain to squirt out of the black hood, and onto the grass. The skeleton's shine, flat black eyes, transparent skin, muscles, ligaments, tendons and organs vanished, as its magical life force dispersed.

Eeklan was startled, and frozen, for a moment, by this eerie phenomenon, then he discarded his bow and quiver and drew the skeleton's sword from its sheath.

"Armed intruders!" a Rider warned. "Turn and defend!"

"Stay close," Eeklan told Mime. "The next blade belongs to you."

"What about the slaves?" another skeleton shouted.

"They're useless to us if we're dead!" the warning Rider shouted.

Eeklan raised his sword and charged into the shallow valley. He lopped the hood and head off the Rider on his left, and crushed its skull with his boot heel.

The rest of the skeleton crashed to the grass and skidded eerily for a few inches before it went dark.

Eeklan chopped off the hood and head of the next Rider to his left, and crushed its skull.

A skeleton to the right advanced on Eeklan's back.

Mime grabbed up the second Slaver's sword, spun wildly around, and cleaved the Rider on one robed knee. The leg snapped in half, and the skeleton pitched to the earth, striking its skull.

Two advancing Riders tripped over their prone comrade. One dropped to its face, unharmed. The other fell on Mime's sword, decapitating itself. The impact pulled Mime to his knees, on the grass.

The two Riders guarding the slaves abandoned their prisoners to defend themselves against Eeklan's deadly assault.

The clangs of sword striking sword rang in the valley.

The horses spooked and stampeded.

The skeleton which had toppled unharmed, angrily regained its footing, snatched up its blade and

charged toward the dwarf.

Two infuriated women threw themselves on the Rider's back.

The skeleton staggered forward, then fell on its face.

The women rolled sideways off the Rider, and struggled to their feet.

The skeleton grabbed its sword, leaped up, and turned on the women.

Mime released his blade, scrambled to his feet, and threw himself against the napes of the skeleton's knees.

The Rider flipped backwards, landing on its shoulders and skull. Its neck broke, and its legs fell heavily across Mime's back.

Eeklan whacked the flat of his blade to the top of a Rider's skull. The cranium shattered and the skeleton collapsed like dead weight; its shine vanishing.

Eeklan slammed the edge of his sword against the temple of another Rider. Its skull flew to pieces inside its hood, and the skeleton flipped over sideways and skidded across the grass.

Eeklan ran to Mime. He crushed the skull of the Rider with the snapped neck. Then he mashed the cranium of the dazed skeleton whose leg Mime had chopped.

Mime shoved the Rider's legs off and stood up. He looked sadly around at the skeletons scattered about the little valley.

Eeklan tossed his sword to the grass.

The women were comforting the frightened children.

Mime strode to the group. "Is anyone injured?" he asked one of the women who had saved him from the Rider.

She brushed her dark hair back from her pale cheeks. "We are all scared," she said, "but no one is hurt." She hugged a small girl to her. "Who are you?" she said. "We thought all men had been captured."

"We have been fortunate," Eeklan said.

The rest of the group crowded around Eeklan and Mime.

"Our men delayed some Riders so we could retreat to safety," a blond woman said, angrily. "But these *monsters* found us."

"We thought we were done for!" another woman sobbed. "Then you came and—" Her eyes filled with fear. "Will you stay with us?" she pleaded.

All eyes turned to Eeklan. "Where were you going?" he asked.

"A hidden valley!" a black haired boy chirped. "My daddy told us about it." Tears brimmed his dark eyes. "Before he—he went to delay the Riders."

"Is it far from here?" Mime asked. He patted the boy on the shoulder.

"No," the blond woman said, "only a couple of

hours. It is surrounded by a woods. The entrance is a tunnel in rock, behind an enormous Larn tree. There are fish and small game there." She fought back tears. "You will come with us, will you not?" she said, anxiously. "Stay with us?"

Sixteen pairs of frightened eyes watched Eeklan. He sighed and looked at Mime.

The dwarf gazed into the night and whispered to himself as though he were distracted by something which only he could see and hear. He touched the dark haired boy on the shoulder. "Has your father taught you how to trap and skin small game," he asked.

The boy smiled, shyly. "He did!" he said. "And I caught a Babbit and cooked it too! Over a fire I made!"

"Good," Mime said. "You other boys, do you know how to fish and trap?"

"Yes," they chorused.

"Did you live in towns or on farms?" Eeklan asked.

"Farms," the dark haired woman said. She wrung her hands. "You are not staying!" she cried out.

Some of the other women started crying. A couple became angry.

"What deeds have you that are more important than preserving our children?" one demanded.

"Remember what you said," Mime asked the dark haired woman, "about all the other men having been captured? It is probably true. Many women are also imprisoned. Monglom wants our children to grow up to serve him, so they are in the work camps, as well." He turned to the angry women. "Eeklan and I are journeying to defeat Monglom," he told them, firmly. "We *must* try."

Mime's voice was so sad, Eeklan wondered how the dwarf could bring himself to speak his next words.

"You must allow us to go. We can escort you to your valley. You will have to care for yourselves, once you are there." He smiled. "You are all from farms. It has not been easy to turn your land into food, has it?"

The women shook their heads.

"You have toiled long and hard before," Mime said. "You and your children have run your farms for days when your husbands were at market. You can care for yourselves in your valley. These young men can hunt, trap and skin. The ladies can fish and find wild vegetables. You have built homes before, too." He smiled again. "You can do it. Will you?"

"How can you fight Monglom if Pourn is dead?" the blonde woman asked. "His magic will strike you down, before you can harm him."

"You felt there was no hope only minutes ago," Eeklan said. "Then we came."

"You must have hope," Mime said. "Desire can often be accomplishment. There are ways to solve almost any problem."

The dark haired woman looked at the others.

Proud determination gradually replaced fear on her face. "If these gentlemen are brave enough to take on Monglom," she said, to her group, "we can shoulder our *own* burdens."

The blond woman glanced down at the swords of the Riders. "Azlin, Ral, Bonn," she said, "gather up those blades. The sheathes, too. We will need them to chop wood for houses, and to hunt." She wiped tears from her blue eyes. "Do you wish one of the swords—Eeklan?" she asked, meekly.

"My bow and arrows should be sufficient," Eeklan said cheerfully. "I am keener with a bow, than with a sword. And a sword is simply too strong a temptation to shave!"

Everyone laughed.

They gathered up the blades, sheathes, belts and habits of the Riders.

Eeklan recovered his bow and quiver. "Lead the way, angels," he said to the women and children. "It *is* your Vale."

***

The Hidden Valley was just as the blond woman had promised. The trees and shrubs around it were so thick, not even the Riders would venture in. A great rise of rock did cross the front of the valley. The concealed entrance was an ancient, hand hewn tunnel.

The giant Larn tree grew so close to the portal, Eeklan could not have squeezed in, even if it were im-

perative.

The women and children were reluctant to see them leave.

"Remember," Eeklan said. "There are no harmful animals in this area. Only little ones that taste good!" He turned to Mime. "Are you sure you would not like to stay, here, with the children?" he said.

Mime snorted. "I am not *that* great a burden," he said. "Besides, if I remained, who would do your *thinking* for you?"

Eeklan laughed. "You see," he told the group. "We can succeed as partners."

They waved and started away the direction they had come.

Eeklan ran back to the group. "Are any of you unmarried?" he asked.

The blonde woman nodded, with a wondering expression.

Eeklan face almost glowed with his smile. "You will not be offended, if I return, with flowers, after this task is performed, will you?" he asked.

The blond woman blushed. "I would like that—Eeklan," she said.

"Your name?"

"Windy."

"I will return, Windy," Eeklan said firmly, and cheerfully, "and you had best be here!"

"I will try."

"Not good enough, my lady!" Eeklan chided, with a smile.

"I will be here, sir archer!" Windy stated. A shy smile lit up her face. "We will *all* be here!" she added.

"I believe it!" Eeklan said. "Good bye!"

The children ran shouting after the archer. Eeklan shooed them back to their mothers and he and Mime departed.

"You are a magician, Eeklan," Mime said. "You turned grief and terror, into hope and courage. They will survive, now."

"Yes," Eeklan said, "they will be all right. But we may never see them again."

Mime noted tears filling Eeklan's eyes.

"What is it my friend?" he asked. "What is wrong?"

Eeklan sighed. "I have gazed upon Windy before," he said. "She lives a few miles from Mislen Town. I have—loved her for a while, but never tried to meet her. I did not feel my wandering life would be good for her." He sighed again. "When I recognized her in the valley, and saw those Riders threatening her, I nearly lost control over the little common sense there is in my head. We are lucky I did not."

"Perhaps you should allow the lady to decide if the wandering life, with you, would be suitable, to her," Mime said.

"If I did that," Eeklan said, with a laugh, "I know just what would happen, if she said yes. I would find the first piece of unclaimed, tillable earth near her home, build a house, and invite her to civilize me. No more gallivanting with the sly game, for old Eeklan."

"Now, would that be so bad?" Mime said, with a twinkle in his eyes.

Eeklan became serious. "I have never desired such a life, more than now," he said. "Yet, I will abandon all hope of it, to destroy Monglom, even if it costs me my *life*. He must not have those women and children!"

"What you did for Windy, and her people, is even more wonderful than I had thought," Mime said, "and our trip, even more important."

They continued across the grassland, growing ever closer to Monglom's citadel.

The moon set, leaving only stars to light their way.

***

Weariness forced them to stop at the far side of a woods.

Mime leaned wearily against a tree.

Eeklan performed a fast check of the area and motioned to the dwarf.

Their best option for shelter was a circular clump of bushes that looked solid, but grew around a hidden grassy clearing.

To avoid tell tale damage, Eeklan slowly and carefully parted some branches, and they slipped into this natural refuge.

Eeklan smiled. The cold North wind was blocked,

so there was no need to build a fire. He laid down on the thick grass and fell asleep.

Mime tossed and turned beside the archer. He could not, in all truth, see how their mission could succeed against the malignant might of Monglom.

Chapter 4

An Accounting in a Graveyard

Monglom hunched on his throne, brooding.

The surrealistic scene had, again, forced itself into his sleeping mind:

The darkness was touched by starlight as he sat on his throne, in the middle of a vast desert of white sand.

A painfully bright light loomed on the horizon, spreading, with frightening swiftness, in all directions. At its center, two faceless men marched relentlessly toward him. Around them, hung the terrifying presence of that abomination Pourn!

The nightmare warned him that Saint Pourn was reaching from Afterlife, in an effort to destroy him, and it gave him the names of the faceless men.

He had meditated on them, and had managed a brief, tenuous, clairvoyant contact with them:

Eeklan; tall, strong, fearless, and clad in green.

Mime; shorter, educated, stern, determined, and clad in blue.

Pourn? Yes, his meditation had revealed Pourn's

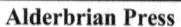

presence around them. It was the unique essence of a soul without a soma.

If Pourn is able to move from afterlife and still retain full use of his powers, why is he trying to contact, and link, with two men?

Monglom was accustomed to thinking in terms of might. This old habit served him well.

Freeing himself from Afterlife drained most of Pourn's energy. One of the men whom Pourn sought was a Mind Medium, a doorway between worlds. Pourn's soul could use him to anchor itself to the Life World. The other man was a psychic energy generator. The first person with such a high yield ability in over three hundred years. Pourn was planning to tap that power.

Could Pourn's damned soul draw sufficient psychic energy from that man to blast through Illkature's protective bubble?

Monglom's heart pumped with fear. Pourn must be certain of the power or he would not be directing his pawns toward Illkature!

Monglom had no choice except to strike the men down as swiftly as he could, and before the link was made. This would cost him the might he could derive from the man who was the generator, but better that, than to lose Langdom, and life itself. He smiled grimly and telepathically summoned the dead commander of his grotesque army.

***

Gray clouds overcast the late morning sky and saddened the woods.

Mime and Eeklan parted the branches of their leafy sanctuary and looked about, with surprise.

A narrow dirt road ran by the bushes and through the woods which lay to their left and right.

There was a wooden post across the road. It had three square signs nailed to it.

The white words on the top sign read: Zaalinn Town. A long white arrow pointed to the right; South.

The second sign read: Zaalinn Church.

The third sign read: Zaalinn Cemetery. A long, white arrow pointed to the left; North.

There was a clearing of grass behind the sign post. The church was nestled there. It was a simple building, painted white. Its peaked roof was shingled with red clay squares. A little porch, shingled with red clay squares, ran along the front. Two white columns stood at either side of the white, wooden steps. There were no windows on either side of the door.

Close behind the church, loomed a woods of red-leafed trees.

Mime glanced from the door, to Eeklan, to the door. "Do you think it is deserted?" he asked.

"The grass is growing over the path to the steps," Eeklan said. "No one has been inside in a week, or more."

"Do you think there is any food inside?"

"We will find out," Eeklan said.

They stepped out of the bushes, crossed the rough road, and climbed the steps.

Eeklan drew an arrow from his quiver and held it like a knife. He turned the knob and shoved the door wide open.

Several small windows in the side walls allowed in the gray light of morning.

The church was beautiful, in its simplicity, but showed signs of neglect.

The ceiling was constructed of arched, varnished rafters.

Dust lay on the floorboards.

The rows of varnished, wooden pews almost shouted abandonment.

The rear of the church was filled by a varnished stage. A tall, white, wooden lectern stood in its center.

As they approached the lectern, their perspective changed, and they noted a door in the far wall.

When they stepped onto the stage, they saw an ancient, leather-bound, holy tome laying atop the lectern, and a high-backed, wooden chair standing behind it.

They crossed to the door.

Eeklan lifted the arrow, turned the knob, and pushed the door open wide.

The Enunciator's living quarters were empty. A cot

stood in the far left corner. A table of unfinished wood and two high-backed chairs sat in the center. A fire-place was to the left of the door; its ashes long cold. A case of books covered half the right wall; cupboards took up the other half.

Eeklan quivered the arrow, faced the cupboards, and rubbed his hands together, hopefully. "Here we are," he said. "I think the Enunciator will forgive us for using his food." He opened the first cupboard, and frowned. "We cannot eat holy books," he said. He opened the second cupboard. "Or cloth napkins," he said. When he opened the last cupboard, it contained only crumbs. "Ah, well," he said. "There are nuts and fruit, and many berries, in the woods."

Mime noticed a narrow closet door behind, and partially hidden by, the open portal through which they had entered. "We might as well make a thorough job of it," he said, wryly. He open the tall creaky door.

A Rider, seated on a wooden stool, glared at them with its flat, black eyes. It was clad in the customary ebony robe and boots, and armed with a sheathed sword.

Eeklan grasped Mime by the shoulders and drew him back toward the rear door of the room.

The skeleton did not draw its weapon, nor did it speak. It stood up, as if inebriated, and stepped into the room.

Eeklan grabbed one of the heavy, high-backed

chairs, and threatened the Rider with it.

The skeleton did not attack. It began to shake, as if suffering a seizure. Its jaw wiggled side to side, in an apparent attempt to speak. Its trembling hand shot to the hilt of its sword. "No!" it shrieked, between its clenched teeth. It took hold of its right hand with its left, to prevent itself from drawing its weapon. "I shall not kill!" it shrieked, with its teeth still clenched.

"What ploy is this?" Eeklan muttered to Mime. He raised the chair to strike the skeleton.

Mime experienced a chill of understanding. He grasped Eeklan's arm. "You are the Enunciator," he said, respectfully.

Eeklan glanced at Mime, with a double take.

"I *was* the Enunciator," the Rider managed to say, through clenched teeth. "My son succeeded me, upon my death, some years back.

"When we marched from Andlon, my birth town, and reached my dear church, I recalled my past. I was horrified by the acts I had committed in Monglom's name. I was at the end of the formation, so I sneaked away, and hid here, to do his cruel bidding, no more!"

"Set aside your chair," Mime said. "He will not harm us!"

"Yes!" the Enunciator screamed. "Yes! I shall slay you! I am given no choice! If you do not submit, to slavery, you must perish! He wills it! It fills my mind, and spills through my bones, enlivening me, impelling me, to do his vile bidding!

"Until your coming, I had stilled his hell within my mind. I was at peace, waiting for my unnatural Life Force to ebb away, and to free me! But now! Now I must enslave you, or slay you! I can no longer fight his abominable, magical instructions!" It jerkily took hold of the hilt of its blade and drew it from the sheath. "Flee!" it begged. "Flee, that I be spared enslaving you! Flee, that I be spared the horror of slaying you! Flee!" It took a halting step toward the archer, and raised the gleaming blade.

Mime grasped Eeklan's wrist and tried to tug him toward the stage door.

Eeklan pulled free and raised the chair to parry the skeleton's sword.

"Kill me!" the Enunciator screamed, with intense despair. "Kill me and free me from his insanity! His evil! Kill me!" It hacked at Eeklan, but only at the chair. It was obvious the Rider was still fighting the influence of Monglom's warped magic. Obvious that it was desperately trying to force Eeklan to kill it, without it being impelled, to harm the archer.

"Give me your blade!" Eeklan roared. "If you wish to be released, give me your blade!"

The skeleton sobbed between its clenched teeth. "I cannot!" it wailed, with heart rending grief. "It is not allowed!"

Eeklan threw the heavy chair aside, grasped the

Rider by its right wrist, and tried to pry the sword from the gloved hand.

It was as if the Enunciator had the reflexes of an animal. It tore its wrist free and raced backwards against the rear wall. It roared like an enraged beast, and charged, its keen sword slicing down like a flash of lightning.

Eeklan ducked to his right, spun behind the startled Rider, and tackled it by the ankles.

The Enunciator hit the floor boards hard, but did not lose its grip on its weapon, and regained its feet almost immediately.

Eeklan had already scrambled up.

Mime charged onto the stage.

Eeklan followed and slammed the door. He grabbed the chair from behind the lectern and jammed the portal shut. He started toward the steps which led down to the pews, but stopped and turned around.

Mime was standing, like a statue, beside the lectern. He was staring at the door to the Enunciator's room.

"What, in the name of good sense, are you waiting for?" Eeklan hissed. "Come with me, now!"

The Enunciator rattled the knob, then howled like a trapped animal. Its sword burst through the thick wooden door, repeatedly, until it could be seen through the resulting damage. "Kill me!" it screamed, shrilly. "Kill me!" When it saw what was keeping it barred from the stage, it shouldered into the thick door, like an angry bear.

The rear legs of the chair slipped free and it skidded, on its back, up against the altar. The sword pitted door slammed open against the wall.

The Rider strode threateningly onto the stage. "If you do not kill me, I will slay you! I will slay you to force your friend to kill me! Help me! For the sake of all that is holy! Help! Slay me!"

Mime's heart ached for the bedeviled holy man. Goose bumps traveled his skin. Perhaps!

"Mime!" Eeklan roared. "Run! Get out of my way! I will split its skull with an arrow!" He was standing between the pews, with an arrow nocked.

The Enunciator raced across the stage, with its gleaming sword pointed at Mime's breastbone. "Damn you, man! Move and allow him to kill me!" it screamed, with ire.

Eeklan cursed and started walking sideways, between two of the pews, to obtain a line of fire that would not endanger the dwarf.

Mime took the heavy holy book in both hands and hurled it at the skeleton.

The Enunciator gasped with horror, dropped its sword, and caught that which it had spent eighty years preserving and worshiping. "Yes!" it shouted, with sudden understanding and hope. "Yes! I see! I was blinded by *his* vileness, but now I see the Light! The Light, of my salvation!" It wrapped its arms around the holy book, and threw its old skull back to stare, with its flat black eyes, at the varnished, vaulted ceiling.

The haunted skeleton began to vibrate, as though it were caught in the epicenter of an otherworldly earthquake. A gray, misty glow enveloped the holy book and spread around the Rider. A low, annoying humming echoed throughout the little church. The good magic, represented by the holy book, and Monglom's evil magic, within the bedeviled Enunciator, were at war. The gray light grew brighter.

"Thank you!" the Enunciator shouted, with joy. "Bless you!"

The humming became a buzzing, which resonated the tragic building. Gray dust shook loose from the rafters of the vaulted ceiling and danced on the varnished floor boards.

There was a brilliant white flash around the holy book.

With a loud retort, the Enunciator, including its apparel and weaponry, burst asunder, into fine, powdery bits.

The holy book fell, undamaged, to the floor, with a thud of finality.

The powder swirled in front of the lectern, for a moment, then dissipated, until there was no hint the

tortured Enunciator had been among the unholy ranks of the un-dead.

Mime picked up the holy book and carefully put it, in its proper place, on the lectern.

"How did you know?" Eeklan asked, incredulously.

"Ours is a religion of positive forces. Benevolent forces. The holy book embodies that. The Enunciator must master control over certain holy healing abilities before he is selected.

"As the Enunciator said, Monglom blinded him to those abilities. The poor Enunciator could have freed himself, long ago, with his own balming abilities, if he had not been so deceived by Monglom's evil. All I did, was remind the Enunciator of this. The poor man did the rest."

"I am glad he is at peace," Eeklan said.

"Amen," Mime said.

"We'd best leave this place, quickly." Eeklan said. He led the way back into the Enunciator's room.

Mime closed the damaged stage door and opened the rear entrance.

White steps faced the Red Woods.

A narrow path pointed to the right, to an out-house.

Mime closed the door.

Eeklan led the way toward the woods.

"It is a shame the church is deserted," Mime said. "It should ring with hymns, sermons, and the laughter of children."

"It will," Eeklan said, "when we destroy Monglom."

Mime tried to laugh. "We have not given thought to how we will achieve that," he said, with worry. "Or even if we *can*."

"I expect we will proceed to Monglom's Illkature," Eeklan said, "recruiting any willing free men along the way. Once there, we can decide upon a plan of action. There is little else we *can* do."

"I wonder if you are correct; if there *are* any other free men," Mime said. "I wonder *if* they will join us?"

"Let us leave that to the future," Eeklan said. "Right now, we had best keep our eyes open for food, and Riders."

They entered the Red Woods, keeping parallel, and close to the road.

***

The church vanished behind.

***

Whinnying startled them. They crept toward the road and knelt behind a line of hedges.

The horse neighed again. It was close.

"Over there," Eeklan said. He pointed to their right. "It is hitched to the gateway of that graveyard."

The gate and the fence were of wood. They were painted white.

"Rider?"

"Doubtful," Eeklan said. "Stories say, Monglom does not allow them to roam, too freely, alone. Besides the poor Enunciator, we have not seen any Riders since last night. This could be a Living. We will risk a closer look. Those trees to our right will cover us."

They inched along inside the woods, parallel to the wide road.

They paused opposite the gateway.

The gate was wide open, toward the road. A dirt path lay between the two equal sections of the graveyard.

There was some movement in the section to the left. They could not discern what.

"There is no more cover until the other side of the road," Eeklan whispered. "Let us cross, quickly, to those Larn trees, to the left of the stallion."

Mime nodded. He checked the road and ran to the indicated place. Eeklan joined him a moment later. They slipped nearer to the fence. A few thin bushes stood between them and the slats.

Eeklan carefully parted the branches. "Damn!" he whispered. "It *is* a Slaver!"

***

The Rider was in the center of that section of the graveyard. It was counting headstones. It stopped, removed its gloves, and stuffed them into a pocket of its habit. It reached into another pocket and withdrew a

small globe of obsidian, which glistened in the light, like a black pearl.

The Rider held the orb in one cupped hand, stared intently at it, and whispered rhythmically.

The Talk-Globe turned blue, then transparent, and a creepy voice spoke:

"Yes, Bamom?"

"I have found another graveyard, my master," the Rider said.

"How many recruits?" the skin crawling voice demanded.

"One hundred adults, my master," Bamom said. "All above the age of nineteen, and below fifty."

"This time, you have performed well," the voice said, icily. "After they are raised, I believe I shall have them guard Illkature."

***

"It is *Monglom!*" Mime hissed. "That horrid, undead, animate *is* speaking to *Monglom!*"

Eeklan frantically motioned for Mime to be silent.

***

"Shall I begin the procedure, my master?" Bamom asked.

"Yes," Monglom growled.

Bamom placed the globe on the fingertips of one hand, and held it above its hooded skull.

Monglom spoke a verse, which not even Bamom

understood.

The ball changed from transparent blue, to gray, and a square beam of black light raised from its crown. The top edges of this ray spread out swiftly, like a clear, ebony blanket, and hovered above the graveyard.

Monglom recited another verse.

The sheet of black energy grew downward, bathing the graveyard in its unearthly glow. The headstones stood out in weird relief.

***

Mime and Eeklan could barely see Bamom.

It stood as if paralyzed.

They heard Monglom intone another rhyme.

The light grew brighter.

They could now see every twig and blade of grass in the graveyard. They were afraid to move.

***

Monglom's voice rang from the globe:

"Come forth! Burst your rotting caskets, and rise! Rise! *I*, Monglom of Aardwicke, Master of Heaven and of Earth and of Langdom, *command* you! *Rise!*"

There was a moment of silence.

The earth began shaking. The grass and ground at nearly every grave was pulverized by Monglom's magic, then it began flowing away from the headstones and into heaps at the feet of the graves, uncovering the coffins.

Monglom intoned a long verse in the old tongue. Intense flashes of gray light illuminated the open graves as he graced the dead with unholy life.

Wood could be heard creaking and snapping as the skeletons forced open the lids of their caskets and began sitting up. Monglom's magic had formed transparent brains, skin, flat black eyes, tendons, ligaments, muscles, a larynx, and lungs for them. One by one, they stood up, until the tiny graveyard seemed packed with them.

Monglom whispered.

His magic gifted the skeletons with Black habits, gloves, boots, belts and sheathed swords.

The earth ceased shaking.

Monglom uttered a final verse.

The ebony light drew up to a flat square just above the hoods of the Riders. It withdrew into a short, square beam of light. This sank into the orb, and the ball became blue and transparent.

"Now!" Monglom shouted, from the orb. "To my Illkature! All of you! To Illkature!"

The skeletons queued in perfect ranks of four. They marched from the graveyard, turning left down the road.

"And me, my master?" Bamom asked.

"You shall gather me more such recruits," Monglom glowered. "If you perform as well again, I shall

gift you fifty years of Magic Life."

Bamom trembled with excitement. "It shall be done, my master!" it vowed, fervently.

Monglom said nothing further.

Bamom rested the globe on a grave marker and searched in its pocket for the cloth bag in which it kept the ball.

Eeklan muttered irately and leaped to his feet. He shattered the fence, with his powerful fists, and hurled himself against Bamom.

The Rider flew into one of the open graves, landing with a thud, forcing the air from its magic lungs; causing an unearthly hiss.

Monglom's voice thundered with unnatural volume through the arcane Talk-Globe: "Riders! Return! Destroy Bamom's attacker! Riders! Return!"

Chapter 5

Shadows of the Beyond

Eeklan hefted a fallen headstone and brought it down on the ball. The globe shattered and the fragments turned black. "You shall not use that augury to thieve our graves again, monster!" he roared.

Bamom leaped eerily from the grave, drew its sword, and advanced.

Eeklan hurled the headstone.

Bamom crashed to its back on the grass and its rib cage and spine were crushed beneath the marker.

Eeklan stamped Bamom's skull to shards, destroying its transparent brain, causing its magic skin, flat black eyes, muscles, tendons, ligaments, organs and life force, to vanish, with a bright flash

Eeklan unbuckled Bamom's belt and tugged it, and the sheath, free. He hooked them around his waist, and picked up the sword. He came back, through the hole in the fence, and took up his bow and quiver. "The Riders will return through the front gate," he said. "We pass this way."

Mime ran with him, left, to the end of the fence.

They paused.

Eeklan checked around the corner, looking left down the road.

The skeletons were running, in formation, toward the graveyard. They turned into the gateway without slowing.

Eeklan and Mime dashed across the road and into the Red Woods. They ran through the trees, going parallel to the road and graveyard.

***

"Fan out!" a high voice ordered, from inside the graveyard. "Groups of five!"

"No!" a raspy voice shouted. "I spied them! They are across the road!"

"That way, with you, then!" the high voice ordered.

The Riders ran through the gateway, across the wide road, and crashed through the woods, in pursuit.

***

Eeklan and Mime delved more deeply into the red hued shade of the woods.

The Riders were catching up swiftly.

One had mounted Bamom's horse.

Eeklan pushed Mime toward a tree. "Climb!" he ordered.

Mime scrambled up the low lying branches and concealed himself in a large crotch.

Eeklan ran to another tree and stood behind it. He

drew an arrow and aimed it along the path which they had taken.

The Rider galloped into sight. None of its comrades were in view.

Eeklan released his bowstring.

The arrow struck the skeleton between the eye sockets, shattering its congenitally weak skull. Its magical skin, flat black eyes, muscles, tendons, ligaments, organs, and life force, flashed out of existence. Its black habit became a heavy bag of bones that flipped backwards off the horse, along with its gloves, weapon, and boots, and landed in a heap, with a clatter.

The frightened steed jumped, kicking its hind legs.

Eeklan dropped his bow and grabbed at the reins, but missed.

The horse bolted toward the road.

Eeklan snatched up his bow. "Get down here," he hissed.

Mime dropped to the dried leaves and struggled to his feet.

They ran farther into the woods.

The Riders were closer now. They were approaching from the left, the rear, and the right.

"At least we are bearing toward Illkature," Mime huffed.

The woods ended at a rolling grass land.

Eeklan skidded to a stop. "Back to the Red

Woods!" he said. "We will just miss the Riders, then follow the far side of the road, in that part of the woods!"

"No!" Mime said. "The grassland! They will never expect it! Too open!" He dashed ahead.

Eeklan followed through the grass, intending to turn the dwarf around.

***

"Have you sighted them?" the high voice called from the woods.

"No!" the raspy voice answered. "If they are not on the grassland, they must have backtracked!"

***

"There is another woods ahead!" Mime said, with hope.

There was a chance. If the Riders were far enough behind, Mime and Eeklan could enter the new woods before the skeletons could reach the grassland.

***

Mime charged between two trees and fell against some shrubs. He sat down, gasping.

"Come on!" Eeklan urged. "We cannot delay!"

Mime struggled to his feet and staggered on.

The woods was extremely thick. Small-leaved Rope Vines grew around the trunks and dangled from the branches, slapping them in their faces as they ran. Briers pulled at their pant legs, and roots and fallen

branches tripped them.

They stopped short.

"A quicksand swamp!" Eeklan said, with frustration.

The mire ran in a long semicircle. One end faced the grassland, the other, the Red Woods they had just fled.

***

Faintly, voices sounded.

"Those rats *have* doubled back!" the high voice said.

"They may have taken to the Gunden Grassland!" the raspy voice said. "There are smaller woods scattered there!"

"Half of you, search the damned grassland, then!" the high voice ordered. "The rest of you, follow me!"

***

"Nowhere to flee, but the grassland," Mime said. "Back into danger. Do we stand, and die?" he asked, desperately. "Or do we surrender, and hope to fight later?"

"We are of no value to Windy and those children, dead," Eeklan said. "Nor, as slaves." He stepped toward the quicksand. "I think these lighter areas are sand over solid earth," he said excitedly. He walked four feet into the sand but did not sink. "Come on!" he ordered. "There *are* land bars here!"

Mime stood next to Eeklan. It was nearly impossible for him to discern the difference in the coloration of the sand.

"There lies a small island!" Eeklan said. "It is sand, over hard earth, also! We might survive this, yet! I'll have to pitch you onto it! Quickly!"

"Are you certain you can make it?" Mime asked, hesitantly.

"No choice!" Eeklan said.

Mime was little comforted.

Eeklan grasped the dwarf by the back of his collar and his belt, and heaved mightily.

Mime landed on his stomach, just short of the oval sanctuary. He clawed frantically at the sandy edges, and began to sink.

"Keep still!" Eeklan ordered. He backed into the woods, ran at full speed, and leaped.

Mime felt the heels of the archer's boots skim his back.

Eeklan landed securely on the tiny island. He spun around, gripped the dwarf by the wrists, and hauled him to safety.

"They *are* here!" the high voice shouted. "*I* was right!"

Boots pounded the earth and fifty Riders emerged from the woods.

"The vermin are trapped!" high voice rejoiced. "Quicksand is behind them! Easy Life!"

They fanned out, drew their swords, and charged, blundering into the quicksand. Clawing and hacking uselessly at the mire, they struggled frantically to free themselves, and screamed for assistance from the other search group of fifty Riders, or deliverance by Lord Monglom.

"I have an unpleasant feeling, once submerged, those Slavers will be able to claw their way to solid ground, and climb out of this quicksand," Eeklan said.

"I suspect they need their lungs only for speech," Mime agreed, "and will not suffocate."

The hooded heads of the skeletons sank into the mire, and the woods fell silent. Their frantic gloved hands, along with their weapons, followed suit.

"Are you ready?" Eeklan asked.

"As you said," Mime replied, dourly, "no choice."

Eeklan heaved the dwarf at the sand bar.

Mime barely cleared the quicksand, but landed safely on his feet.

Eeklan performed another running leap. He hit the edge of the sand bar, held onto Mime's shoulder for balance, and jerked his foot from the quicksand.

The deadly mire began bubbling and seething.

***

Faintly, the raspy voiced Rider could be heard:

"When we reach that woods, ten of you circle to the left around it, ten of you circle to the right! The rest of you, with me, through the middle, until we meet our commander!"

***

Mime and Eeklan stared at the quicksand.

Fifty swords snaked eerily out of the mire near the edges of the pits, and fifty black-gloved hands clawed at the solid ground, just as the canny archer had predicted.

Eeklan and Mime were beyond fear.

They had escaped death, only to face it again, from two fronts. Their single option was to run along the swamp, toward the Gunden Grassland, hoping for a miracle.

***

When their hooded skulls breached the mire, the Slavers angrily tossed their swords onto solid ground so they could use both hands to extricate themselves.

Raspy voice and its twenty-nine companions charged into the clearing, took stock of the situation, and began hauling high voice and its forty-eight comrades free of the relentless quicksand.

***

The brier patches and trees thinned.

"Look!" Eeklan hissed. Tears of hope sprang into his eyes. "A gulch!"

Their legs felt like lead and their lungs ached, but they pushed their bodics, ncarly to the limits of their endurance, and scrambled down into the ravine.

***

Ten Riders rounded the edge of the Quicksand Woods. If one glanced left, it would discover the gulch, and the subjects of their search.

***

Mime sank to his knees in the grassy ravine, trying to control his breathing.

"We cannot rest *now*!" Eeklan gasped. "When those Slavers realize we're not in the far side of the Quicksand Woods, they will head for the grassland and find this gulch!"

"Oh, God!" Mime managed to say. "I wish Pourn were here to help us!" He tried to stand, but could not. His legs were too tired.

Eeklan lifted the dwarf in his arms.

The archer's years of pacing game had served him well. His stamina was superior to most. He began stumbling along the twisting ravine.

***

"They must be in this damned gulch!" the raspy voice shouted.

"After them, then!" the high voiced Rider said, harshly.

***

The sky was still overcast with gray clouds.
Morning wore into afternoon.
Not a breeze stirred.

The grass on the gulch floor gave way to clumps of weeds, and scattered rocks.

Eeklan pushed himself on. He could not afford to slacken pace.

***

"When will these vermin falter?" the high voice shouted. "They move as if they are of *our* ranks!"

"I suspect the big man is a hunter, with unusual strength and stamina," the raspy voice shouted. "Only our Lord Monglom knows about that dwarf!"

"Occult demons, then!" the high voice shouted. "Faster! They will tire, *sometime*!"

***

Eeklan was reduced to a fast walk.

Mime was breathing more easily. "Put me down," he said. "I can walk again."

Eeklan complied. He did not stop plodding because he was afraid if he paused he would collapse. He had never been so fatigued even when chasing fleet game.

"Eeklan!" Mime warned. He grasped the archer by an elbow and tugged him back down the side of the gulch.

Eeklan shook his head, trying to clear it. He realized he had been climbing out of the ravine. "We've to rest," he mumbled. "Can't think straight. Sight's blurry."

"Wait," Mime said. "There is a fork ahead." He peered down one of the prongs, barely able to see its far away end in the dusk. The other prong seemed to have no end.

Eeklan was resting against the side of the main gulch. He was almost asleep.

Mime jostled him.

Eeklan's eyes flew open and he jerked his head up.

"This direction," Mime said.

Eeklan pushed away from the comforting side of the ravine, and stumbled along.

***

"Faster! Faster!" the high pitched voice urged. "We will lose them in the dark, if you do not move, faster! We dare not *fail* Lord Monglom!"

The sounds of footfalls veered to the left, toward the dead end fork, then died out.

***

The gray clouds made evening black.

The winding fork ended at a gentle incline. They climbed out of the ravine and fell to the grass.

Eeklan knew they should not stop yet, should push on, to place as much distance, as possible, between the Riders and them, but his body rebelled. His muscles were numb.

Mime lay still nearby. His mind was so fogged by fatigue, he could not even consider their safety.

Sleep easily overcame both men.

***

Eeklan snapped his eyes open and stared at the blue sky. The dour gray clouds were gone and the golden sun of morning gently warmed him. With a grimace, caused by sore muscles, he slowly sat up.

Mime was gathering Kears from a tree a few feet away.

Eeklan thought it strange the tree should be alone in the center of the grassland, but dismissed it.

Mime brought over an armload of Kears. He sat next to Eeklan and they devoured the golden fruit in famished silence. They had no idea where to go for help. They were certain they were fortunate to be alive.

Eeklan threw his Kears stems over his shoulder, as was the custom. He gazed across the grassland. "Life always seems sweeter after one has narrowly escaped death," he said.

"It does," Mime agreed.

"Not that I have often fled death," Eeklan added.

"Or sought to," Mime agreed.

Eeklan sighed. "Who do we turn to when our leaders are dead, or imprisoned?" he asked.

"I guess, we depend upon ourselves," Mime said. "We performed very well against those Riders at Elpton," he added. "And, against the Riders, in the little valley. And, you were heroic, last night. But, to free an entire world, from the grasp of Monglom!"

"We cannot manage, alone," Eeklan said.

"If we could but journey to Pourn's home," Mime said, sadly. "We should find knowledge, among his tomes on Magic, that should aid us. But no one, perhaps, not even Monglom, knows where Pourn's home lies. Books concerning Pourn, say he kept its location secret."

"More the pity for us," Eeklan said.

The leaves of the Kear Tree rustled.

Mime and Eeklan looked at each other, with alarm.

There was no wind to stir the tree; the grass did not wave!

A thick mist billowed from the ground, enveloping the Kear tree. A stone tablet appeared just outside the mist. Words formed in the slab:

Magician's homes are often not
where one would think they'd be.
Of Mountains, Hills, or Deserts,
Swamps, or Fields,
Valleys, Dells or Underground,
the place not mentioned, is the one.
The greatest one, in truth.

The tablet faded away, then the thick mist cleared, and the Kear Tree could be seen again. Its leaves no longer rustled.

"Who could have conjured this message?" Eeklan

said.

"Perhaps Pourn is not really dead," Mime said, hopefully. "It may have been *him!*"

"If he were *alive*, why would he need *our* help?" Eeklan said. He shook his head. "No," he said, "Pourn is dead. This message comes from someone else."

"Or *somewhere* else!" Mime whispered. "Perhaps Pourn is speaking from the grave."

"His powers were great," Eeklan said, uneasily, "but to do this, from the Shadows of the Beyond—impossible! It is *someone* else!"

"Perhaps it is Monglom, then?" Mime said.

"Why would *he* dispatch this message?" Eeklan scoffed.

"To trick us into the hands of his Slavers?"

"Do you really think Monglom would waste so much magic, just to gain two more slaves?" Eeklan said. "Wouldn't he leave that low task to his officer Riders?"

"No other magician, on Langdom, besides Monglom, could do this," Mime insisted. "It if was not the Twisted One, then, it must have been Pourn's *soul!*"

Eeklan winced at that disturbing argument.

"Pourn is probably dispatching a like missive to every free man and woman on Langdom," Mime suggested.

"Good," Eeklan said. "Somebody is bound to find the correct site. Let us see if we can be the ones. The

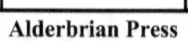

one not mentioned," he mused.

Mime mentally repeated the words of the message. He shrugged.

"Mountains, Hills, Deserts, Swamps, Fields, Valleys, Dells, or Under Ground," Eeklan said. He thought for a moment, then snapped his fingers. "He did not mention Lakes, Streams or Rivers!" he exclaimed.

Mime nodded his head, in excited agreement. "It is *Nalan Lake!*" he said. "That is the greatest body of water on Langdom!"

"An island," Eeklan said, happily. "That must be it!"

Mime stood up. "There are bound to be commercial ferryboats at the shore," he said. "We can commandeer one of those."

"I know the fastest way, to Nalan Lake, from here," Eeklan said.

Chapter 6

A Resurrected Pourn?

The tall thick blades of the grassland slowed their trek toward Nalan Lake.

Mime drew closer to Eeklan.

"There are Riders near here," the dwarf said.

Eeklan said what Mime had not.

"Yes, they have frightened the game birds away. Wild horses roam these lands. The Riders are most likely gathering mounts for their increasing ranks."

There was a howl like an angry cat.

"Clayeagle!" Eeklan warned. He shoved Mime down, and threw himself into the grass.

The huge, green fowl swooped toward them. Its claws were extended, and its red eyes were gleaming, fiercely. It made a tight circle, left, and soared up. It dived again, almost catching Eeklan's bow in its sharp talons.

Eeklan rolled onto his back and nocked an arrow.

The bird swooped a third time.

Eeklan took careful aim.

An eerie whistling sounded.

The Clayeagle shrilled an answer and abandoned its attack, swerving to the left. The arrow missed it by several feet.

"Damn!" Eeklan whispered. He got to a crouch and stared after the fierce fowl.

Mime cautiously got to his knees.

There was a lone Rider approaching, several yards to the left. It was astride a black stallion, which it reined to a halt.

The eagle alighted on the Rider's hooded skull.

Eeklan's arrow arced in the sky and plunged into the soft earth.

The skeleton issued a wavering whistling.

The enormous bird hove into the sky.

The Rider drew its long broadsword and reigned the snorting stallion toward the site from which the arrow had originated.

The Clayeagle would spy Mime and Eeklan no matter how they tried to hide in the grass. It had to be dealt with first.

Eeklan nocked and released another arrow, which pierced the Clayeagle's heart. The bird howled and collided with the skeleton, causing both to tumble to the grass. The Clayeagle lay, dead, atop the Rider.

As the spooked stallion passed Eeklan, he grabbed his bridle, soothing him with gentle words and tone.

The skeleton angrily rolled the Clayeagle aside. It retrieved its sword, scrambled to its feet, and charged.

"Eeklan!" Mime warned. "The Rider!" He rushed forward, seized Eeklan's bow up, and struck it against one of the skeleton's booted ankles.

The Rider fell on its face. The rush of air forced its hood backwards, revealing its gruesome head to the sunlight. The blade flew free of its black gloved hand.

Eeklan snatched up the sword and stood astride the skeleton. He brought the blade down, splitting its half raised skull, from crown to chin, and snapping its neck. He took the hilt of the sword in both hands and thrust the blade, through the rib cage, deep into the ground.

The Rider shuddered, once, and lay still.

"That was *too* close," Eeklan said, with relief. He shook Mime's hand, then shouldered his bow.

"We have a horse now, though," Mime said.

"And more company!" Eeklan warned. He pointed beyond the dead eagle.

Seven mounted skeletons were galloping to their fallen comrade's aid. Through their transparent flesh, their teeth and skulls glinted in the sun, looking like white fire, under the shadowy halos of their ebony hoods.

Eeklan mounted the nervous stallion and pulled Mime up behind. He heeled the steed into movement. "We shall serve them chase, for their swords!" he said.

"Make it good!" Mime alerted. "They have another Clayeagle. Probably, the dead one's mate!"

Eeklan's stomach knotted. If the Clayeagle he had

slain *was* the live one's mate, they were in worse trouble. The bird would follow them to the ends of the earth to avenge the demise of its spouse. Not even the Riders could control it, now. He turned in the saddle. "Have you ridden much?" he asked.

"Yes!" Mime replied.

The stallion attained a full gallop.

"Take the reins, while I dispatch this bird!" Eeklan said.

Mime reached his short arms around Eeklan's waist and took control of the steed.

Eeklan un-slung his bow and nocked an arrow. He nearly lost the shaft.

The headless Rider struggled to its feet. With its left palm, it shoved the tip of its sword even with its chest. With its right hand, it pulled the sword from its back and sheathed it, by touch. It bent over, felt around, and picked up its head. It placed the halves together and cradled them in the crook of its left elbow. One of its comrades reined up beside it, and Split-skull mounted behind.

Damn, Eeklan thought, I failed to realize that skeleton didn't lose its magic life and flesh like the others I slew. You really do have to *shatter* their skulls, to make sure they are dead! I won't make *that* mistake *again!*

The Clayeagle vented its angry cat howl.

Eeklan returned his attention to the huge fowl. It

was about a hundred yards behind. There was even more reason for him to be sure to hit his mark; the beast now had their scents. He raised the bow and loosed the jagged tipped missile.

The Clayeagle seemed to anticipate the arrow's release. It bobbed up, then down, caught the shaft in its claws, snapped it in half, and allowed the pieces to fall.

Eeklan nocked a second arrow. He aimed and shot, almost in a single motion.

The bird did not realize it. The shaft plunged into the fowl's green chest. It howled, and its wings faltered, but it forced itself to continue the chase. It was only a few feet above the grass.

"Damn! Damn! Damn!" Eeklan said. "I have heard how tough these flying monsters are, but never believed it, until now!" He nocked a third arrow, aimed and shot. He nocked a fourth shaft, in case it should be necessary.

The Clayeagle was weakened from loss of blood. It was unable to swerve. The arrow tore into its heart and it tumbled to the grass, dead.

Eeklan released the fourth arrow, which stuck in the lead Rider's forehead, knocking it off balance backwards. The terrified skeleton clung desperately to the reins to avoid falling to the ground and being trampled. The horse assumed the Rider wanted to stop, and did so, post haste, kicking up clumps of grassy earth, and blocking the paths of the other skeletons.

Eeklan shouldered the bow and took the reins.

Mime looked behind. "The Riders are all down!" he shouted, jubilantly. "Except the skeleton whose skull you chopped! It is running after us!"

Eeklan chuckled. "Our bony friend wants another pair of legs, and a long tail, before it can hope to compete with this fine steed!" he shouted.

"His friends do not! "Mime shouted. "They have gotten up and are after us again! How far to that lake?"

"Just a bit farther than you can spit a sow," Eeklan said.

The archer reigned the stallion down a steep slope, then around a clump of crimson-leafed trees, and toward a small, green woods. Nalan Lake lay beyond this, glinting blue-green in the sunlight.

"Can you spy the Riders, now?" Eeklan shouted.

Mime glanced around. "No!" he shouted.

"This is a fine time for a trick my father taught me," Eeklan shouted. He left the saddle, pulling Mime after him. They hit hard, and rolled breathlessly, until they came up against an old log, near the little woods. Eeklan struggled dizzily to his feet and dragged Mime into the grass, under the WideLeaf Trees.

The stallion quit the grassland, for the sand of the lake shore, then veered back to the grassland.

Eeklan checked the beach to the right. There was

an old rowboat lying at the edge of the water. It was upside down. He hauled Mime out of the woods and up behind the weathered boat.

***

The Riders appeared at the top of the grassy slope. They thudded past the woods, following the deep tracks of the fleeing stallion.

***

Mime and Eeklan exchanged relieved smiles.

Eeklan checked his bow, quiver and sword.

"My thanks to you," Mime said, wryly. He was tired of being dragged about like a side of meat. "My congratulations to your father."

Eeklan inspected the rowboat. "He was an able man," he said, "and very clever. He sired me, did he not?"

"I shall not hearken to such rude wind!" Mime said. "Let us launch this dubious craft before they return and make fools out of us and your clever, if reckless, father."

Eeklan snorted at Mime's comment and heaved the boat onto its keel. The oars were tied down under the two seats. Eeklan pulled the craft toward the water.

Mime resolutely pushed the stern.

"I shall fashion a warrior out of you yet," Eeklan grunted.

"If I do not turn you into a teacher, first," Mime huffed.

"Ugh," Eeklan gasped.

Mime was not sure if it was in response to his comment, or the effort involved in moving the boat.

***

The flat black eye caught a movement on the lake shore. Split-skull stopped running through the knee-high grass. It lifted the left side of its head into the air with its left hand. It turned the skull-half until its eye centered on the movement. It was the two escapees pushing a rowboat toward the water! For the first time, with excitement, Split-skull noted: the tall man wore green, the short man, blue!

***

Mime took the seat in the bow of the boat, facing the lake. Eeklan sat down on the stern seat, with his back to Mime, untied the long oars, set them into their oarlocks, and began rowing across the placid expanse of water.

***

Split-skull placed its head together and cradled it in the crook of its left elbow. It ran as swiftly as it could in the direction its companions had taken in their pursuit of the riderless horse.

***

The other Riders met Split-skull as they returned to the beach. They had the panting stallion in tow.

Split-skull placed its head onto its neck to use its

ersatz lungs. "We have been made to look like idiots, a second time," it said, angrily. "Our quarry has taken to the water. I believe they are the two men our master most desires!" It turned its skull to a skeleton sitting astride a gray mare, and said, "Have you the Talk-Globe, still, Taglog?"

Taglog twisted around, rummaged in a saddlebag, and brought out the ball of black obsidian. It cupped the orb in outstretched hands and recited an incantation, as Bamom had.

A gray fog surrounded, then entered the ebony orb. The ball became blue and transparent, and the mist inside vanished.

Monglom's gaunt visage appeared and mirrored interest. He knew his slaves had not had time to gather the horses he required. They would not risk his wrath with trivial matters. "Speak!" he commanded, with his skin crawling voice.

Taglog's hands shook.

The orb trembled, but Monglom's image stayed steady.

"We have spied the two vermin you are seeking, master," Taglog said.

Monglom looked surprised. "I did not expect them to bear this far West!" he said.

"They have taken to Nalan Lake in a rowboat," Taglog said. "They are—"

"Heading for Pourn's Island!" Monglom roared. His face became pale with fear and rage. "This *traves-*

ty must not be!" he shouted. "With his magic favor, from beyond the grave, they can succeed in passing through the protection field of his stronghold, where I could not. *They must not do so!*" With his right hand, he lifted his Talk-Globe, and held it close to his gaunt face. "I *must* destroy all chance of this crime happening; be rid of Pourn's Castle, *forever!*"

Taglog gasped, then spoke, in spite of its terror of its vile master. "But, Lord, you will also destroy the secrets vaulted there. The magic knowledge—"

Monglom's eyes burned with hatred. "Yes!" he shouted. "It is better to lose those treasures, than to be faced with a resurrected Pourn! This is what *will* happen if his servants enter his home! I may not be able to defeat him *again*; to slay him *again*! He would be forewarned, *this time!*" He balanced the Talk-Globe on both palms, and breathed out a spell.

The Riders could not understand the words.

Monglom's globe transmitted, to the sphere of the skeletons, a picture of the window that faced the dome and the black mountains outside Illkature.

Monglom spoke a second indecipherable rhyme.

The Riders watched in awe.

The mountain chain released a great rock slab. Monglom coated this with the gray glow of his evil energy and floated it toward the dome. As it traveled, the slab wobbled, wavered, and transformed into a three masted, ebony schooner.

The gray light vanished.

Monglom recited another verse.

The Riders still found the words unintelligible.

The schooner began shrinking, passed through the energy dome, and sped toward the palace. When the ship sailed through the window, to hover before glowering Monglom, it was half the size of the orb, he grasped in his wrinkled hands. He flicked a finger, and the schooner entered the Talk-Globe.

Taglog's Talk-Globe switched from the view of the glassless window, back to Monglom. He leaned forward on his throne and held the orb in outstretched palms. The tiny schooner hovered serenely inside.

There was a smile on Monglom's gaunt face which frightened the skeletons.

"With this arcane ship, shall you obliterate Pourn's Stronghold, and murder his witless puppets," Monglom ordered. He whispered a fifth spell.

The schooner emerged from the Riders' orb, like a ghost passing through a window, and hovered above them.

Monglom breathed a sixth rhyme.

The ship began to regain its original size.

Monglom repeated his terrifying smile. "Board the vessel and heed your orb," he commanded. "It will direct you as to my wishes."

Taglog's Talk-Globe returned to solid black.

Chapter 7

The Howling Vortex

Pourn's Island arose on the horizon.

"Beautiful," Mime said, leaning forward, and staring intently.

Eeklan ceased rowing and looked over his shoulder.

The vegetation was bright green and tropical in nature. Multicolored flowers grew everywhere except the beaches. There were silver birds wheeling in the air but their calls could not yet be heard.

Eeklan resumed rowing.

***

They slowly neared the shoreline.

"Look," Mime said, pointing.

Eeklan stopped rowing to see.

In the center of the isle, there was a small mountain. Halfway up, they saw a bright, purple gleam.

The waves carried them closer to the island.

The purplish glow became more distinct. It resembled a low, transparent, upside-down bowl. There was a darker purplish structure inside.

"The Fortress of Pourn," Mime whispered, with awe.

The gentle waves beached the craft on the white sand.

Eeklan jumped from the old boat and dragged it beyond the reach of the lapping water. "There are no other tracks in the sand, so no one has been *here* recently," he said. "But, someone could have landed on the far side of the island, and climbed the mountain, from there."

Mime did not take his eyes off the stronghold.

Eeklan shouldered his bow and quiver. "Shall we see what our protector Magician has waiting for us?" he said, cheerfully.

"Yes," Mime agreed. "Wholeheartedly."

They trudged under the afternoon sun. The sand gave way to grassy hills, which ceded supremacy to rocky, cracked earth. This led straight to the base of the mountain. A long flight of steps was cut into the white stone. They took a gentle incline toward the bubble.

A flock of Bane birds swooped in from the far side of the island. They began circling the men, playfully.

Eeklan paused on the steps to watch. Four birds perched on his shoulders. He raised a hand to shoo them, but two more alighted on the back of it. They cocked their heads side to side, inspecting him, curiously.

Mime was distracted from the wonder of Pourn's palace. He laughed at his friend's predicament.

"Fiend!" the archer scolded him. He gently tried to shake the birds off his hand. He was unsuccessful. "I

hope these friendly feather balls pluck you bald for their nests!" One of the Banes on his shoulder rubbed its tiny head against his neck. He recoiled, with a laugh.

"They must sense the similarity between the size of their brains, and yours," Mime said.

Eeklan hissed, in mock anger.

The Bane birds darted out over the lake and began circling in a frenzy, flashing silver in the sunlight.

A chill coursed down Mime's neck and spine, then seized his heart. With panic, he whirled around to look at Pourn's Stronghold. "No!" he screamed, and began running up the white steps.

Eeklan clenched his hands at his sides.

The gleaming schooner hovered, like some deformed beast, high above the purple bowl. The eight skeletons had abandoned their robes and were manning the various stations of the ship.

Taglog stood astride the captain's aft deck with the Talk-Globe balanced on the fingertips of one hand. It pointed its other forefinger toward the part of the mountain above and behind Pourn's purple bubble and lifted the ebony ball high.

There was a moment of deadly silence.

The Talk-Globe shone with a gray light almost as bright as the sun, then Taglog's forefinger emitted an intense bolt of lightning, and the top of the mountain exploded, burying Pourn's Stronghold beneath tons of roaring rocks and swirling dust.

Mime screamed with despair and collapsed on the steps as though he were dead.

Taglog looked toward the dwarf.

"Mime!" Eeklan warned. He charged up the steps, two at a time, and gathered his limp companion into his arms. He checked his bearings, then spun around and fled.

Forks of lightning crackled from Taglog's forefinger.

The steps behind Eeklan were melted into puddles of white, smoking slag. A tongue of lightning licked the stone in front of him. He leaped across where the step had been, and ran even faster down the stairs. A bolt of lightning melted the rock behind him. Another strike exploded a section of the earth between the steps and the cliffs beside him. The concussion sent him sprawling onto the dirt between the steps and the side of the mountain. The unconscious dwarf was spilled from his arms.

Lightning speared into the earth near Mime, kicking up dirt and heated stones.

Eeklan rolled to his knees and snatched up his bow. Lightning burned past his left ear and exploded a hole in the mountainside. Dirt and stone chips showered into the air.

Eeklan nocked, sighted and loosened an arrow, almost in one motion. It struck the center of the Talk-Globe, shattered it in half, and impelled the pieces overboard.

Mime sat bolt upright. He darted his eyes about, for a confused moment, then scrambled to his feet.

The schooner was swinging around and descending for the kill.

Eeklan and Mine raced down the remaining steps, crossed the short, rocky Piedmont, climbed over the grassy hillocks, and trudged through the white sand, to the rowboat.

Eeklan tossed his bow and quiver into the craft. He tugged the stern, and Mime pushed the prow, toward the water.

The silent schooner blocked the sunlight, creating a cool shadow, and began a ponderous descent toward its prey.

With all his strength, Eeklan pulled the rowboat across the last of the beach, and into the water, too quickly.

Mime lost his grip on the prow and fell on his face, slightly stunned by the impact. He sucked in a breath and rolled over, and over, and over again.

The great ship settled to the sand, with a horrible crunching.

The tail of Mime's shirt was caught under the prow and he was pinned down. Eeklan grabbed it free and they scrambled into the bobbing rowboat.

Mime took his seat in the bow, facing the stern, as Eeklan began rowing.

Two skeletons drew their swords, jumped from the

black deck of the schooner, to the wet white sand, and waded into the water.

Eeklan's prodigious oaring had taken the rowboat beyond reach.

The angry Slavers were forced to turn back.

Two Riders tossed a rope net over the side of the ship. Their comrades scrambled up, and the schooner began to rise in pursuit.

Mime grabbed Eeklan's big bow, and nocked one of the remaining arrows. But, what good was that; he could not draw the string back far enough to send the shaft where he desired! He recalled a trick he had seen at an archery contest. He fell onto his back and placed the toes of his boots against the inside of the bow. With both hands, he drew the arrowed string to his chest and pushed his feet forward, locking his knees. His body trembled with the tension of the bow, but he managed to raise his legs, sight hastily, and release the string.

The arrow struck Taglog square in the right ankle, knocked its foot out from under it and flipped it, forward, off the aft deck. It flailed its arms and uselessly grabbed the helmsman skeleton. The helmsman lost its grip on the tiller, and both Riders tumbled to the main deck, in a macabre heap.

The schooner was at the mercy of the air currents. It began swerving right and left and bobbing up and down. It wobbled slowly away from the quarry, back toward Pourn's Island.

"Canny shot," Eeklan said to Mime. He stopped rowing and stared in amazement.

Split-skull was perched on one of the schooner's thin, black railings. It clutched its skull in both hands, raised it high over its shoulders, and leaped for the rowboat. With an expression of utter frustration, it realized it had grossly misjudged the distance, and hurled its skull at Mime. The halves fell into the water on opposite sides of the boat, then the body plunged in feet first, and Split-skull was no longer a threat.

Eeklan resumed his hasty rowing.

Taglog and the helmsman had untangled themselves.

The angry helmsman took hold of the tiller and regained control of the vessel. It swung the schooner around in a wide arc, and aimed it toward the rowboat.

Mime groaned. "We are in for it, now," he said. "My first shot was lucky. And we have only *three* arrows left." He looked at Eeklan, desperately. "Did your father teach you any more tricks?"

Eeklan ceased rowing and stared toward the afar island, his face creased, with disbelief. "Pourn?" he said. It was more a question, than a statement.

A chill tingled down Mime's spine. Pourn's Island was obscured by a glowing purple waterspout, bearing toward them, with alarming speed.

The schooner, lashed by spray, began heaving up

and down in the increasing winds. The black masts bent in a frightening manner, and the ebony stone sails shimmied.

Eeklan seemed to divine where the spout was not going. He rowed the boat to his left, pulling as hard as he could against the oars. The shaft of his right paddle cracked in half, and he lurched to his left.

The roaring of the waterspout became almost deafening.

Mime and Eeklan jerked their heads up.

The waterspout enveloped the schooner, and tore at it, using mighty wind hands. With a frightful, repetitive, cracking sound, the sails broke off, flipping through the air like pieces of colored paper, the masts snapped, and the body of the vessel split into several boulder-sized sections. Skeletons, swords, and rope nets, were hurled into the churning water.

Taglog rode triumphantly astride the aft deck as this largest portion of the shattered ship plummeted toward the rowboat.

Eeklan and Mime covered their faces with their arms and cried out in panic.

The great, jagged rock slammed into the spray-topped lake, just in front of the creaking rowboat. This created a rolling wave behind Mime which swept the ancient craft into the howling vortex of the waterspout.

The rowboat spun crazily around the rim of the

whirlpool, growing slowly closer to its center, and disaster.

Mime and Eeklan clung, fearfully, to one another.

"The oar!" Mime shouted, urgently, into Eeklan's ear. "Throw the oar, through the side of the spout!"

"What?" Eeklan shouted. "Why?"

"I don't know!" Mime admitted. "But, do it! *Now!*"

Eeklan hefted the heavy oar from its oarlock. He prayed Pourn was behind Mime's idea, then hurled the paddle into the wall of whirling water.

The spout parted along its towering, roaring length, and, the rowboat shot out of it, skimming wildly across the waves. The spout repaired itself, and spun off, toward Pourn's Island.

The mainland seemed to appear out of nowhere. The creaking rowboat crashed against a short expanse of sharp, gray stones, and splintered to pieces. Mime and Eeklan were thrown up and forward. Their impact with the white sand beach rendered them unconscious.

Chapter 8

The Lights of Invisibility

Monglom awoke in stark terror. He sent his psychic energy forth, filling the air with bright, grayish light, and sat up in his ornate, ebony-marble bed. He darted his wild eyes around the bare, black walls of his secret room, twice, before he could squelch the fright.

"So," he muttered. "Pourn's Stronghold *is* buried. But, it has cost me *eight* of my cleverest Slavers!"

He threw the satin bedclothes aside, swung his feet to the cold floor, and stood up. He recited a verse. His attire changed from his gray sleeping-robe to his black day-robe and boots. He mentally commanded the flush door to swing open long enough for him to stride into the cavernous audience room. He climbed the high dais and seated himself, regally, on the ostentatious throne.

"Damn Pourn!" he swore. "I did not think he had established the link to his puppets! Now, it will be almost impossible to kill this Mime and Eeklan!"

He pounded an arm of the throne. Pourn followed the correct path, he thought, irately. The Natural

Path. Pourn's abilities *will* last, *forever*!

"I will never be able to reach out from Afterlife," he muttered. "My psychic abilities will end with my death because my talents depend upon the powders my slaves mine. But, if I can prevent Pourn from utilizing the man who is the psychic power source, my drugs will keep me alive, and in command of Langdom, indefinitely."

I need not alter my scheme, he thought. I will bend every effort, as quickly as possible, to locate and liquidate this Mime and Eeklan. The place to begin, is the northern shore of Nalan Lake!

***

Eeklan regained consciousness. He blinked at the yellow sun and clear blue sky, and sat up on the sand. The countryside was splotched by forests. He sighed with relief. Mime was nearby, and breathing. He collected his arrows, quivered them, and shouldered the quiver. He took up his bow and tapped one tip against the dwarf's shoulder.

Mime came awake instantly. He rolled up to his knees and stared wildly around for a moment. He glumly stood up. "What do we do now," he said, "since we cannot utilize Pourn's books?"

"Pourn has aided us twice," Eeklan said. "That waterspout required a lot more power than sending us the stone message. Do you suppose Pourn has regained his might?"

"No," Mime said. "Pourn might be a little stronger. But, if he had his powers again, he would not need us. He could defeat Monglom, alone."

"Maybe he is slowly rebuilding his might to full strength," Eeklan suggested.

"He still would not need *us*," Mime said. "Not now, that his Stronghold is buried. He probably had an aid to recharging his energy, in his Citadel, and required us to perform some action to activate it. Now, he will have to proceed more slowly. We do not know how long it will take him to regain full might. Or, *if* he *can*. And, we *cannot* assist him."

"Yes we can!" Eeklan exclaimed.

Mime looked hopeful. "How?" he said.

"We can seek other magicians who may be able to tell us a way to help Pourn's soul increase its power."

"Surely, every real magician has been captured, by now," Mime said.

"Do you *know* of any magicians around here?" Eeklan insisted, gently.

"There is, one, that I have heard of," Mime said.

"Lead me to his home," Eeklan said. "If he is there, no matter how weak it is, we will find some way to make his magic be of help."

There were old farms scattered among the grassy hills and the forests around Nalan Lake. Mime and Eeklan passed through many of these.

All were silent and deserted.

***

They stopped at one of the abandoned farms. They found stale bread in the house, and drank from the well, which stood in the front yard. They leaned against the winch posts.

"Monglom will soon have our people slaving on this farm," Eeklan said. "Monglom!" He spat out the name as one would utter a foul word. "How can he commit such crimes against our people?"

"According to History," Mime said, "and I am not defending him, the powders which Monglom takes, altered his personality. They destroyed his conscience, impaired his morality, and exaggerated his lust for power. It is believed the drugs control *him*. I can not imagine a worse fate."

Eeklan shook his head. "Nor can I," he said. "But," he added, "did not Monglom know, before hand, those powders would pervert his thoughts?"

"Writings say, experts warned him of such side effects," Mime said.

"Then, there is no excuse for his actions, and no pity for him, in my mind," Eeklan said.

"It is written that Monglom did not believe the experts," Mime said, quietly. "Even though the monks showed him people who had suffered insanity because of the drugs."

"Did Monglom believe himself to be so superior, he would be unaffected by the twisting of the evil powders?" Eeklan asked. "Or was he merely, stupid?"

Mime laughed, almost convulsively. "You banged the nail head securely, twice, that time," he said.

Eeklan looked momentarily puzzled by Mime's reaction. Then he smiled. "Come," he said, "let us be about our task."

"It is still a long way to the magician's home," Mime said. "It is in a forest town."

They left the rest of the farm fields and struck out across the hilly, forested landscape. Each man was deep in brooding thought.

Bright day gave way to lengthening shadows. The hot sun turned crimson as it set, pulling down a sullen curtain of twilight in its inevitable trip beyond the edge of the world.

***

The full moon lighted the sky with white. Mime and Eeklan stopped atop a hill. Below them, the town of wooden buildings formed a large circle. It was difficult to tell whether the Riders had been there.

***

Mime and Eeklan paused, uneasily, at the main street. They heard no hint of life. There were no lights in any of the structures, and all their shutters were closed.

The nearer they came to the center of the town, the darker it became.

Mime glanced at the sky. The moon was obscured by thick, black clouds. He shivered, as if it were winter. With men like Monglom, he thought, one's worst fears became reality. "A taste of things to come," he mumbled.

"Did you say something?" Eeklan whispered.

"Just to myself."

"Look," Eeklan said. "Here is an inn."

It was a dilapidated, two story, clapboard building. Eeklan marched to the portal and knocked.

There was no response.

Eeklan rapped harder.

Someone inside moved about.

Eeklan banged on the door.

A frightened man said, "Go away! Leave us alone!"

"Open up!" Eeklan ordered.

"The place is full!" the man said. "Now, go away and leave us in peace! Go away! Do you hear? Go *away!*"

"Ask about the magician," Mime urged. "Armell."

"Do you have a magician here?" Eeklan shouted, angrily, at the door. "A man named, Armell?"

"Not here," the man said. "On the other side of town. At the edge of the forest. Now, leave us, *please.* Go bother *him*, if you like. *But leave us be!*"

"Let us visit the *magician*, Mime," Eeklan said, huffily. "Maybe *he* will treat *us*, in a *civil* manner!"

The rest of the town was just as quiet and dark as

the inhospitable inn.

**

The forest began where the town ended.

Almost in the grasp of the towering trees, the huge, weathered, clapboard house was as dark as all the others, and its eroded shutters were just as tightly closed.

They traveled a dirt path, to the brick front steps.

Eeklan admired the expensive, gold-colored, star-shaped knob, as he rapped on the door.

There came no response.

Eeklan knocked again, much louder, and the door swung open, inward.

Eeklan and Mime entered, with caution.

The long hallway was dimly illuminated by a line of white, glowing rectangles affixed to the middle of the sky blue ceiling.

There was no one to greet them.

The door swung softly shut.

Mime and Eeklan turned around, warily.

An old man in a dark blue robe stood there. He was tall, balding, and wrinkled. He bowed his head, as a courtesy. "Welcome to the humble dwelling of Armell," he said, his voice solemn. "I have been expecting you. We have little time." He showed them down the hall and into a large library furnished in deep blue. The walls were lined with shelves.

Mime marveled at the number and antiquity of the

books.

There were two armchairs, upholstered in blue velvet, with their backs to the hall doorway. A huge, brown desk, and another blue-velvet armchair, set before the rear wall. To the left of the desk, stood a dark blue door. A wooden chest sat beside this portal, and against the left wall. A fireplace, in the right wall, filled the room with cozy warmth and a cheery, golden light.

Armell seated himself on a corner of the fine desk. He gestured to the armchairs.

Mime and Eeklan settled into them.

Armell smiled, sadly. "I have glimpsed the future," he said. "I saw only a small part of a scheme involving thousands of people. Something prevented me from viewing every detail." He leaned forward, earnestly. "This I saw, most clearly: the coming of two men to ask of me a special question, the fall of this town, and my capture, by the Dark Riders."

"Surely, you can prevent this!" Mime protested.

"The one who has conceived this plan is far more powerful, than I," Armell said. "I can do nothing, but wait. My time *is* coming, and I cannot escape." He shrugged, sadly. "I have warned the townspeople but they are much too frightened to do anything except cower behind locked doors. As if *that* will protect them!" He raised a hand, to forestall any comments. "What is your question?" he said.

"We believe Pourn's soul is reaching out from Afterlife," Eeklan said. "He has aided us twice in our fight against Monglom. We want to know if you possess any knowledge that could help Pourn recharge his might, and perhaps, even return to life."

Armell became angry at himself. "My life's mission," he said, "has been the search for an artificial method of gaining abilities such as those of Pourn and Monglom. It has been to no avail. I know nothing which can do this, besides Monglom's drugs, and they destroy the user." An expression of urgency crowded his face. "There is only one way in which I can aid you," he said.

He stepped to the chest and lifted the lid, leaning it back against the wall. He took two torches out and handed one to each guest. He sat on the corner of the open chest.

"What good are torches?" Eeklan asked, with irritation. "If we lighted them, the Riders would see us for miles." He started to lay the torch aside.

"With them lighted," Armell corrected, patiently, "the Riders will not be able to spy you, even inches away."

"What?" Mime exclaimed. He held his torch as if it had become hot.

Armell smiled, proudly. "I have developed these torches. When lighted, they, their flames, and whoever carries them, become invisible. Even the heat of

their fires is not felt by one not holding such a torch. Nor is the smoke smelt.

"Each man who wields one of my torches can be seen by anyone who holds a similar torch. He can also bend the magic so that any man he chooses who is not wielding such a torch, will see him. Each torch bearer can become visible, just by the thought of it. They will enable you to stand beside Monglom, himself, *if* you are truly *determined* to *resist* him." He paused and raised a warning hand to his lips.

There was a faint sound of hooves on packed earth.

Armell strode to the fireplace, pulled a burning stick out of the fire, and returned to his desk. "The Riders come for me," he said. "You must leave. It is my *fate* that I go with them." He lit the torches.

Mime and Eeklan vanished from sight.

The horses thundered to a stop outside the front door. They could be heard snorting and restlessly stamping their hooves.

Armell tossed the firebrand into the fireplace and quickly opened the back door.

Mime and Eeklan reluctantly fled.

A Rider heeled its mount around the house, to guard the rear door, a moment after Armell closed it.

Mime barely dodged the steed's hooves.

He and Eeklan ran into the darkness of the forest.

***

The lead Rider dismounted in a clumsy fashion and raised its gloved hand toward the gold-colored, star-shaped knob.

Armell opened his front door. "Welcome," he said, with a smile. "I have been expecting you."

The Rider, startled, stiffened for a moment, then grasped the magician by the shoulders and jerked him into the night. "Monglom wishes to, *entertain*, you," it rasped.

"*I* know," Armell said. He climbed, with dignity, astride the skeleton's steed. "*I* am ready," he added, haughtily. "You may now, proceed!"

This tall, old man is unnaturally serene in the face of his capture and enslavement, the Rider thought. It was very much afraid of Armell. After all, it reminded itself, ruefully, he *is* some sort of *magician*. It mounted, rather warily, in front of Armell, motioned for its twelve companions to follow, then heeled its horse along the side of the house. It called to the rear guard and led the party in the direction in which Mime and Eeklan had fled.

Chapter 9

Psychic Storm

Mime and Eeklan were deep in the forest.

"Listen!" Eeklan warned. He stopped and looked behind.

"What is it?" Mime said. He was afraid the magic of the torches had failed.

"I hear horses," Eeklan said. "It must be the Riders who were at the magician's home." He pulled the dwarf behind a clump of bushes. "We will let them pass," he said.

"Why hide?" Mime asked. His fear was increasing. "Do not our torches function, any more?"

"A precaution," Eeklan assured, softly. "The more careful we are, the longer we will survive."

The Riders appeared from the blackness. They passed within feet of the hiding place.

"Armell!" Mime whispered, to Eeklan. "They *are* taking him to *Monglom!*"

The Riders faded out of sight.

"We will never be able to catch up with them and help Armell escape!" Mime despaired.

"We must think of all of Langdom, rather than one man," Eeklan reasoned, sadly. "Maybe we will be able to find him, once we destroy Monglom."

"*If* we destroy Monglom," Mime corrected. "*If.*"

"With these fine torches to conceal us, we stand a much better chance, than before," Eeklan said, "even without Pourn. We need only to advance within arrow range of Monglom, and—"

Mime was cheered by this thought. "Yes!" he interrupted. "With your eye, the Evil One's fate is as good as sealed!"

***

The forest ended in less than a hour.

They pushed on, trying to get as far across the open grassland as they could before they were forced to stop for sleep.

***

More massive black clouds began to gather around the moon. They looked like twisted faces pressed against one another.

The wind picked up, fluttering the yellow flames of the torches.

A fine rain began to fall.

Eeklan called a halt. "We will have to seek shelter!" he shouted, over the hum of the wind.

"Back to the magician's house!" Mime shouted.

"No!" Eeklan shouted. He took hold of the dwarf's

wrist and pulled him along. "The heart of the storm is about to pass over us! His house, and the forest, are four miles back! There should be a woods, closer than that, ahead!"

Mime knew the archer was more at home in nature. He allowed Eeklan to tug him along.

Lightning flashed, blue-white, above.

Thunder shook the earth.

A gust of wind sent Eeklan flying sideways. His hold on Mime was broken, almost as if by strong hands. His torch was knocked from his grasp as he slammed into the ground, and the flames were nearly extinguished when he snatched it off the wet grass. He lurched to his feet, and glanced around.

Mime was gone!

Eeklan searched frantically for a glimpse of his friend's torchlight, but sighted nothing. How far was I blown by that strange wind, he wondered. He cupped a hand around his mouth, to be heard above the sounds of the wind and lashing rain, and called for Mime.

He concentrated, in order to turn off the magic of the torch. This was so Mime could see the flames, in case the dwarf had lost the second torch. He had to trust, to Armell, that the mere thought, would make him visible.

It began to rain harder.

Eeklan waved his torch, in a wide arc, over his soaking head. He could see only a few inches beyond the glow of the flames. A frightening realization came to him, almost as if a warning voice had whispered in his ear. Monglom was doing this!

Eeklan's heart began pounding with apprehension. He shouted, at the top of his lungs, for Mime, and ran in the direction he thought Mime was.

Several bolts of lightning erupted overhead, the thunder shaking the ground even more.

Eeklan caught sight of the flickering of Mime's torch. He realized the dwarf must have switched off its magic. The flames were faint, and they were circling, with frightening speed, some feet above the sodden grass.

"How can this be?" Eeklan said. "Unless—" He ran harder.

The illumination from the lightning faded and Mime's torch glow vanished in the darkness and rain.

Monglom dispatched his gale across the tall grass. Its unnatural force smashed into Eeklan's face and chest.

Eeklan leaned into the gale, and struggled toward where he had seen the light of Mime's torch.

Monglom stopped the gale.

Eeklan stumbled.

Monglom spun the archer around with the gale and dashed him to the wet grass.

Eeklan lay on his chest, weak and panting. His torch was jerked from his unsteady hold and broken in two, as if by invisible hands. The halves were hurled

so far into the night and the rain, that the flames vanished. His bow and quiver were pulled off his shoulder and flung into the dark.

Mime screamed in the distance. It was barely audible over the sounds of the storm.

Eeklan forced himself to draw a deep breath. He stood up.

Monglom speared a cross wind at Eeklan.

The archer struggled against it, slowly gaining ground.

Lightning erupted, ground up, only yards ahead of Eeklan. It blinded him temporarily. The concussion of the thunder knocked him to the grass.

Monglom's wind rolled Eeklan, side to side, back to where he had originally lain.

Eeklan's ears and brain rang from the punishment. "Mime!" he said, feebly. "Please—" He gasped. The rain was drumming on his back, like falling pebbles. "Pourn!" he cried out, with despair. "Please! Somehow! Help us!"

A clap of thunder shook the earth, followed by another, and another.

Several tongues of lightning, directly overhead, lit the grassland like midday, followed by even louder thunder.

Eeklan caught a glimpse of a weak, flickering, yellow light. He fought his way to his feet. "Mime!" he shouted. "I am coming, Mime!" Then, as if threatening anything in his way, "*I am coming!*"

Monglom used his psychic gale in an attempt to spin Eeklan around in a circle.

Eeklan braced himself against it.

Monglom began to buffet him with the gale.

Eeklan was overcome with rage. He drew his sword and sliced at the magic wind. He charged on, making some headway.

Monglom increased the force of the gale.

Eeklan was stopped. No matter how furiously he struggled and hacked against the gale, he could not move ahead. "Pourn!" he screamed. "Please! Somehow! Help us!"

Pourn dispatched his energy.

The sword came alive in Eeklan's hand and pulled him along as if the occult gale were no longer blowing.

Lightning flashed behind, and Eeklan's shadow stretched weirdly across the grassland. Ahead, before the light of the bolt faded, he sighted Mime in the rain fogged air.

The dwarf was still clutching the wildly flickering torch. He was whirling and jerking around, about twelve feet above the matted grass! It looked as though Monglom was trying to tear the dwarf apart with his magic winds.

Pourn tugged the sword until Eeklan stood beneath the dwarf.

Mime appeared to be unconscious. His free arm

flailed. A strange voice issued from his lips. It was clear and strong: "I shall take care!"

Monglom increased the force of his winds. They tore the sputtering torch from Mime's hand, snapped the stick in two, and hurled the halves into the stinging rain.

Pourn pulled Eeklan's arm back and then flung it forward. The sword flew into the air and hovered above Mime. The blade emitted a brilliant white light, illuminating the ground for several yards.

Monglom made his magic winds hurl Mime toward the earth.

Eeklan cried out, in panic, darted forward, and caught the dwarf in his arms. Their heads butted, and the men tumbled to the soaked grass, unconscious.

Monglom set his magic winds for the kill. They swirled clockwise into a spout, like a crazed beast chasing its tail. Then he directed it to suck the quarry into its vortex.

Pourn increased the light of the sword until it was blinding. He spun the blade in the sky counterclockwise, absorbing the force of the murderous winds. As the magic winds were abated, the shine of the blade decreased. Soon, there was only the hovering sword, the darkness, and the gentle, natural rainfall watching over Mime and Eeklan.

***

The rain ceased and the first gray light of dawn showed in the East.

Eeklan woke slowly. He managed a sitting position. The sharp pains were gone, but his body ached.

Mime moaned. He rolled onto his back and stared into the clouded sky.

Eeklan crawled over and looked down. "My father used to say, any storm that can blow you flat, is a storm to walk away from. But he never did tell me how."

Mime grimaced. "Perhaps that was because the one storm your father turned his back on, to walk away from, took half of his mind with it, when it left. The half with the sensible answers." He flexed his sore arms and stood up.

Eeklan considered what his friend had said but shook his head. "We have had a good taste of Monglom's might," he said. "And another look into Death's black eyes."

Mime only nodded.

The clouds uncovered the orange face of the sun. The light began to warm the travelers.

Eeklan checked his sheath and looked about for his bow and quiver. "We must find my weapons," he said. He wrung rain from his shirt front.

"And before the Riders are upon us," Mime said.

Eeklan scowled. "This fine sunrise makes all that happened, seem like a nightmare," he said. He squeezed water from the back of his shirt.

His sword dropped to the grass by his feet. He and

Mime jerked their heads back and stared at the sky. The last of the black clouds had blown away. A few birds glided on the gentle upper breezes.

Mime gazed at the blade. It was reflecting the sun in a normal manner. "We have had another example of the magic of Pourn," he whispered. "He continues to protect us. That is why I was not torn to pieces last night." He paused, thoughtfully. "I have a dim recollection of what occurred, but—did Pourn speak through me?"

"Yes."

"What did he say?"

"I will take care."

"But, why?" Mime wondered.

"He still needs us, for something."

"I know why!" Mime said, with a shiver. "In a very ancient book on ghostly phenomenon, I read that, in cases of unexplained actions—knocks on walls and flying dishes—someone nearby gave the spirit its power.

"I am the medium, through which Pourn can work in our Life World. You are the power source, the amplifier. He uses most of his might to channel through me, and needs you to enable him to combat Monglom.

"The strangest aspect is, Pourn is doing this now and we cannot tell it. This is why he is protecting us!"

"Does that mean Afterlife cannot draw Pourn away, against his will?" Eeklan said.

Mime frowned. "No," he said, with worry. "The

same book says Afterlife exerts more might than we can imagine. There is no guarantee Pourn will not be withdrawn from Langdom, for some otherworldly purpose, by whatever rules Afterlife."

"We cannot depend on Pourn being with us, always," Eeklan said, a bit gloomily. "We can only hope so."

"Yes. Another thing. Since Pourn requires us for power and mobility, he can not reach far beyond us. That is why we will have to face Monglom with Pourn."

"Then we shall!" Eeklan said. "I cannot believe the powers in Afterlife want any thing but Monglom's destruction. I will gamble our Pourn will be about whenever we really have need of him."

"I am sorry," Mime said, "no bet. Afterlife is an enigma, even to those who write about it. The Death World's rules are not always logical, or even reasonable, to us." He appeared more hopeful. "But, that which we believe is just, does appear to be so, in Afterlife. Monglom's defeat *is*, just."

Eeklan smiled. "Then, you do believe Pourn will be with us, to the end?" he said.

"It is possible—"

"We still should not plan on it," Eeklan finished.

"How I wish we could," Mime said. He lifted the sword and handed it over. "We must not leave this," he added.

Eeklan slipped the blade into the sheath. "There is

no telling how far my bow and quiver were blown," he said.

"Nor," Mime reminded, "how soon the Riders will arrive. We had better move, with haste." He gestured toward the distant, great forests of the South, then to the continuing grassland, to the North. "Which way?" he said.

Eeklan turned to the North. "To Membling Pass, and our friend Monglom, of course," he said. "But first, to find my bow." He faced South and began searching.

Mime fell into step beside the archer. "How are we going to reach Monglom's palace unseen by the Riders, now that we have lost our torches, and our element of surprise?" he asked.

"Element of surprise, huh?" Eeklan said. "And I thought you were not a warrior!"

"I am not," Mime said. "My head is not thick enough!"

"No," Eeklan said, with a laugh, "but it is big enough!"

Mime chuckled. "Enough of this," he said, "we must give our attention to our search."

"A good chortle," Eeklan instructed, "has helped many a beleaguered man." He cawed, with delight. "And it ofttimes heightens my ability to observe."

He stepped to the right, to a clump of bushes, and returned with both quiver and bow. One end of the quiver's strap had come unbuttoned from the pouch. It had wrapped itself around the string of the bow and had been carried by the storm wherever the bow had been blown. During its flight, the quiver had lost one of its three remaining arrows.

Mime pressed his fingers against his eyes. He recalled they had received only two or three hours of sleep. He patted Eeklan just below the shoulder. This was as high as he could reach. "First, we must find a safe camp," he said. "Then we must sleep, so we will be better able to help our people."

Eeklan nodded.

They plodded, tiredly, toward the North. Only grass lay before them.

***

They stopped at a field of corn. It was the only cover, for as far as the eye could see, in all directions. The golden stalks grew very close together.

Eeklan frowned. The corn was wild and inedible.

They spread corn leaves atop the stalks and settled down, in the shade, under this roof. It was close quarters, and the earth was damp, but they were hidden from cursory viewing.

***

Mime and Eeklan awoke simultaneously.

Voices, and the thudding of many hooves, sounded nearby.

Eeklan drew a half moon in the earth, to indicate the Riders.

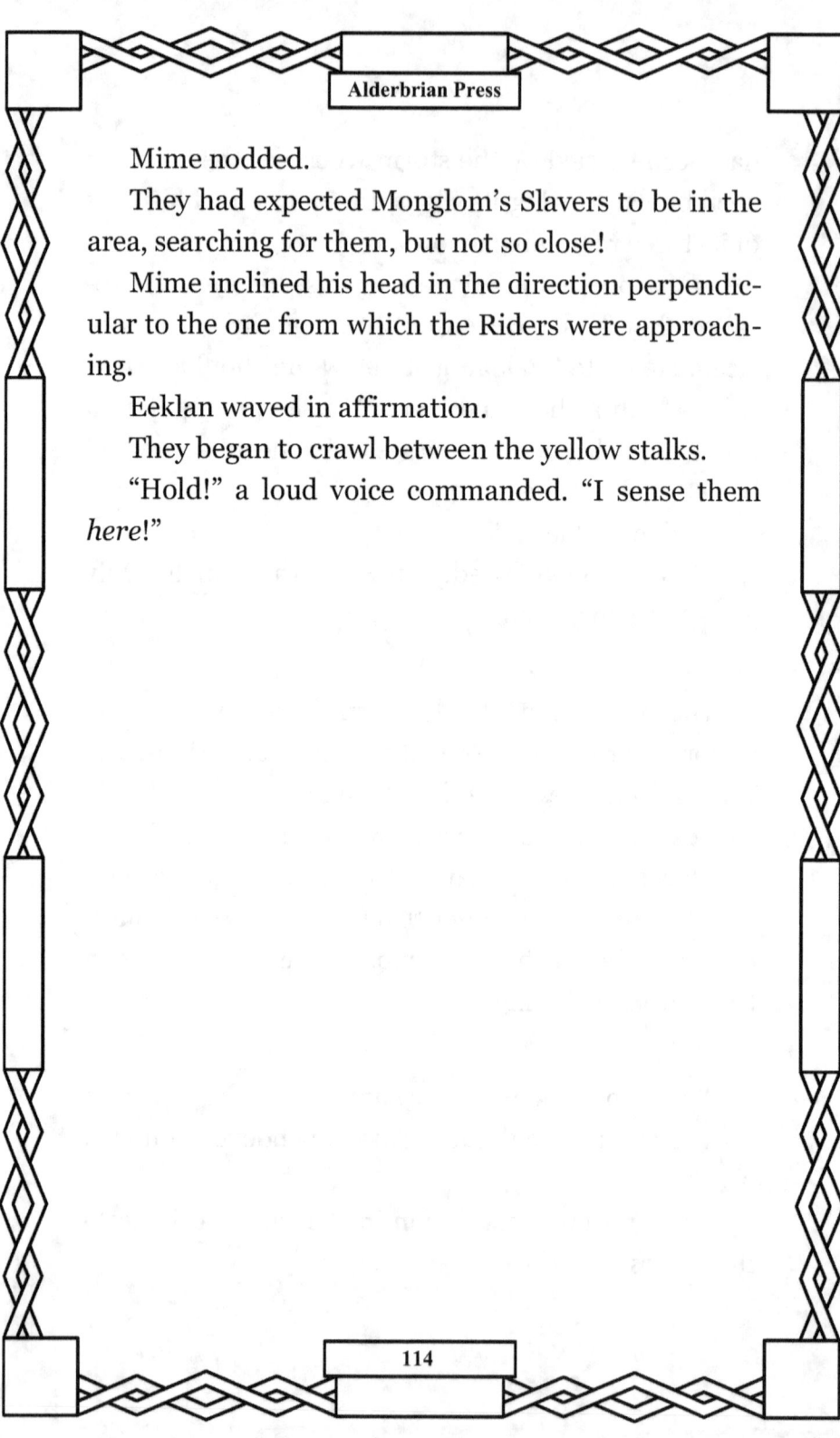

Mime nodded.

They had expected Monglom's Slavers to be in the area, searching for them, but not so close!

Mime inclined his head in the direction perpendicular to the one from which the Riders were approaching.

Eeklan waved in affirmation.

They began to crawl between the yellow stalks.

"Hold!" a loud voice commanded. "I sense them *here!*"

Chapter 10

Approach the Yellow Light

Eeklan and Mime lay motionless, stunned that the Riders could sense their presence.

The hooves thudded relentlessly closer.

Monglom has been attacking us since we attempted to reach Pourn's Isle Stronghold, Mime thought. Now he has endowed his evil Riders with the ability to divine our position. I hope Pourn will be able to overcome this new obstacle.

The Riders were almost upon them.

"Pourn has failed to intervene," Eeklan whispered. "Prepare to fight!"

"No!" Mime whispered. "Follow me! I see a light!"

"What?"

Mime struggled to his feet, and fled through the corn stalks.

Eeklan knew it was futile to try to outrun mounted pursuers, but he leaped up, and followed.

"There they are, the imbeciles!" a Rider shouted to its six companions. "They might have edged past me, if they had stayed quiet. Now we have them!" It heeled its horse after the quarry.

Eeklan lost sight of Mime!

"Hurry!" Mime whispered, urgently, from just feet ahead. "I have found a way *out!*"

Eeklan feared the dwarf was too terrified to think straight. Only more wild corn lay before him. Frustrated, he followed his friend's voice and the ground disappeared from under him.

Eeklan landed beside Mime inside a large hole which was illuminated by no discernible source.

Eeklan looked up, in fear. The Riders would be upon them in moments! His fright turned to wonder. A shimmering, transparent barrier covered the mouth of their burrow.

***

The Riders thundered directly over the hiding place. They quickly returned, and spread out, in a second search of the corn field. In a few minutes, they regrouped above the burrow.

Mime and Eeklan could see and hear the Riders.

To the Riders, the shield looked like a normal section of corn field.

"I cannot sense those vermin anymore!" one of the Riders said, angrily. "Monglom's magic is working, but I have lost them!"

"Never mind," another skeleton said. "They must have used conjury to elude us. That means they are the men we seek. Monglom will be pleased to hear we have spied them. His *magic* will destroy them for us."

"All right," a third Rider said. "Stop the talk! It would have been nice to receive Triple Life for them, but we must return to the main party and report to Monglom by the Talk-Globe. At the least, we have earned the Life Boost we need!"

The Slavers grunted in accord and galloped west.

***

Eeklan stared at Mime. "How did you know this place was here?" he said.

"It was as though a lighted arrow pointed the way," Mime said. "It is Pourn again! He is still warding over us!"

Eeklan nodded, eagerly. "It looks like your theory is correct, and we have a constant ally," he said.

"Well—" Mime began.

"Surely, if the eerie laws of Afterlife would stop Pourn," Eeklan said, quickly, "he would not have been able to come through, in the first place. He did, so it stands to reason, Afterlife approves of Pourn's battling Monglom."

"Or, it has not discovered what Pourn is doing," Mime countered. "But, if what you say is correct, then —if you were faced by an equal enemy, how would you defeat him?"

"Do the thing least expected, of course. And, while that enemy is frozen with surprise, conquer him. Why?"

"Monglom is more or less Pourn's equal," Mime said.

"So, whatever Pourn has in mind," Eeklan said, "it will be a surprise, to Monglom, you mean."

"To us also, I fear. I am not sure I like not knowing what Pourn plans to involve us in."

"Whatever it is," Eeklan said, "Pourn will keep us safe."

Mime smiled. "We hope so," he said, "or Windy will be a widow before she is wed."

"And you may receive some notable lumps not caused by Monglom," Eeklan retorted, with a grin. He closed his eyes to rest for the danger that surely lay ahead.

Mime settled back against the dirt wall of the burrow. He shivered in the damp coldness and watched the white wisps of a wind broken cloud drift across the afternoon sky.

***

Mime grunted.

Eeklan lifted his head and looked at his companion. "What lurks in your mind?" he said.

Mime hesitantly raised a hand toward the odd, clear barrier. He did not touch it. "I have been thinking," he said. "Why does Pourn keep us here for so long?"

"He sees more than we can ever hope to," Eeklan said. "Those foul Riders may have returned and may be searching the area around our corn field. Or there may be some other danger he sees."

Mime's face showed insight as he stared at the shield. "You are wrong," he said, "Pourn does not keep us here because of outside threat." He lifted his fingers toward the barrier. They trembled slightly. "We keep ourselves here by not leaving." His hand passed through the shield. He stood up and climbed out of the burrow.

Eeklan shook his head in astonishment and hoisted himself up onto the ground.

They turned to look at the hiding place. It was no longer visible.

Eeklan cautiously pressed a foot where the shield had been. The earth felt soft and normal. He adjusted his quiver and bow on his shoulder.

They began to walk North.

"It seems we cannot succeed without Pourn's protection," Eeklan said.

"I know," Mime said. "That is why Pourn will do his utmost to stay with us."

They crossed the field of wild corn into another grassland dotted with small woods.

***

Afternoon lingered to evening. The grass began to thin. The earth grew damp, then muddy, then covered with water. The water rose to their ankles, and the flora changed to brown reeds.

***

The night sky was alive with stars. Their blue-white light reflected brightly from the water, creating sharp shadows. These made shapes and distances seem larger than they were.

The further into the dim marsh Mime and Eeklan ventured, the more chilly it became. The only sounds were the ones they made by striding through the water.

"It is longer across than you estimated," Mime said.

"And wider," Eeklan said.

"This water seems to be rising, by the minute," Mime said. "Is it wise to continue?"

"Even if it does reach our waists," Eeklan said, "it is better to wade across, in a few hours, than to trudge around, in one or two days."

"Are you certain there are no harmful water—Look!" Mime said. He pointed.

They could discern a black shape ahead. It was a woods.

"Those WideLeaf Trees look strange," Mime whispered.

"Yes," Eeklan agreed. He motioned for a halt. "That is it, they are in a perfect circle!"

"Some one has planted them, you mean?"

"And, long ago," Eeklan appraised. "Eighty years, or more, according to their height."

"Why are you studying them?"

Eeklan's smile was just visible. "Have you noticed how the star light is not reflected as brightly nearer the woods?" he said. "It is because the water is less deep there."

"The woods is dark, so the trees are on land," Mime said. "Dry land?"

"Probably."

"A possible campsite for us?" Mime ventured.

"We will find the far side of the woods. If the rest of the marsh looks too big to cross before sunrise," Eeklan said, "we will get some sleep here."

"I thought the center of a marsh was where the water was always deepest," Mime said. "But that circle of trees is in the center. Is it possible—"

"Monglom?" Eeklan interrupted. "No. You see those two rills on either side of the woods? See how the starlight is reflected really brightly there? This is because that is where two underground springs emerge, flooding their waters away from the woods. There must be a third spring behind the woods, to cause that distant reflection, beyond the trees."

"It is a dim reflection," Mime said. "Which means, there is not much of the marsh behind the woods."

"Right."

"I think it prudent to camp for the night, whether the marsh has ended on the far side of the woods."

"We will see," Eeklan said.

They approached the woods cautiously.

The chilly water did give way to dry land. There was some moss around the tree roots, but little else. The highest branches of the WideLeaf Trees created a thick, dome-like canopy. Not even a glimmer of starlight was visible through their leaves.

Eeklan touched Mime's shoulder and pointed.

There was another ring of WideLeaf Trees before them. There was a faint, yellow glow in the center.

"Rider outpost?" Mime asked.

"Not likely," Eeklan said. "Outposts require visibility. From where the light appears to be, there is no view of the territory surrounding the marsh. It is obvious, whoever is in there, does not want to be discovered. He has gone to great trouble, to mask his light."

"Should we investigate?"

"No," Eeklan decided. "We cannot indulge in curiosity this close to the Harlan Wastes. We will skirt around the woods and seek shelter after we have left the marsh." He started to retrace their steps.

Mime gripped the archer's forearm.

"What is it?" Eeklan asked.

There was no response.

A white light enveloped Mime's head. His face showed fright. His lips were trembling and his jaw was jerking up and down.

"Do not fight it," Eeklan said. "It is Pourn trying to speak, to tell us something."

Mime realized Eeklan was probably correct. His fear subsided and he relaxed.

"Remain in the woods!" Pourn said, softly but sternly. "Approach the yellow light!"

"Why?" Eeklan asked. "What is there?"

There was no reply.

Pourn's white glow vanished.

"He is finished," Mime said. "I hope he does not possess me, again, without trance. Trance is like sleep. This—this was like a seizure."

"Were you harmed?" Eeklan asked.

"No," Mime said. "Just very annoyed and startled. There must be something useful at the place with the yellow light, or Pourn would not order us to it."

They moved gingerly into the second ring of trees. After perhaps three minutes, they saw that the yellow glow was emanating from a hut constructed of tightly woven reeds. They heard movement inside and stopped in front of the reed door.

Eeklan made a circle with his thumb and forefinger. He looked through it at Mime, and motioned for him to wait.

Mime nodded.

Eeklan started around the hut.

Mime cried out.

Eeklan ran back to the door.

The outside of the portal was covered by a white light. It was vaguely man shaped. It wavered momentarily, like a reflection on a rippling pond, then detached itself from the door and stood before the hut.

Eeklan dropped to his knees. "Pourn," he whispered, reverently, "you have come to us."

Chapter 11

Battle of the Haunted Hut

The misty white light brightened. It formed into a tall oblong. Violet tinged it. "No," it said, with a shrill, angry voice, "not Pourn!" It gradually became an incredibly old man dressed in a yellow robe. His hair was white and long, his snowy eyebrows bushy. His eyes were pale blue; his nose small. His lean face was a mass of wrinkles. His feet were bare. He grew more solid in appearance. The violet light faded. "No," he repeated, "I am not Pourn. I am one who lives with his own company." He turned to the door.

"You are a magician?" Mime said, hopefully. He reached out to catch hold of the old man's hand, but his short fingers passed through the image's wrist as they would through a warm mist.

The old man whirled around. The purple anger light haloed his head. "No, no magician," he said. "No magician. Only one who has developed special abilities, special tricks, in his old age." He faced the door and wavered through it.

The woven reed portal swept open inward. The

floor of the hut was packed earth. The old man waited just beyond the doorway. He remained enveloped by the glossy white light, but the purple glow was gone. "Come," he invited. His voice was still high, but no longer shrill with anger, as it had been, when he was mistaken for Pourn. "I will shelter you for this night."

Mime smiled at the old man and entered the structure.

Eeklan took a last look around the brooding trees. He saw no threat, but still felt ill at ease as he went into the hut. The first thing he noticed was the stench of decaying flesh. Then he saw a half rotted corpse lying on a grass mat in the far corner.

The old man paid no attention to the body.

There was a shallow pit in the middle of the floor. A small log fire burned there. An iron rod lay beside it.

The old man picked up the rod and stirred the fire. The red light of the flames could be seen through him.

Eeklan darted his eyes from their happy host to the corpse. He grasped Mime's shoulder. "The body!" he whispered. "It is him! This is a, *ghost*, Pourn has guided us to!"

"I know," Mime said, soothingly, "but the *ghost* does not."

Eeklan let his hand drop. "What?" he said.

"A person does not always accept death," Mime said. "This discarnate does not. Which is probably why Pourn has brought us here. This man was likely a friend, and Pourn wishes to aid him in passing into Afterlife."

"Pourn intends to *exorcise* him?" Eeklan said, uneasily.

"Yes," Mime said. He gestured for silence.

The ghost laid the rod beside the fire. He frowned. "How rude of me," he said, "I have left the door open, and you might catch a chill. It gets cold on the marsh, at night. But I am used to it." He flickered, and the energy of his thoughts swung the door shut. He held his hands out, indicating the earth by the pit fire. "Please, be seated," he said. "I have no furniture, besides my mat, as I seldom have guests." He settled down cross legged, near the fire.

Mime and Eeklan sat facing the discarnate, with their backs toward the door.

"Thank you for allowing us to share your home," Mime said.

The ghost smiled with pride, making his face look more wrinkled. "You are hungry," he said. It was a statement, rather than an inquiry. He floated to his feet and walked past his body. A leather pouch, with a long drawstring, hung from a peg in the wall.

"We must humor him until Pourn begins the exorcism," Mime said. "We must not spark the ghost's anger. Now that he is dead, he possesses psychical powers, and will use them to fulfill his rage."

"I expect Pourn will keep him from harming us,"

Eeklan said. "I wish he would do something about the stink."

Their host took the pouch down and looked into it. He closed the pouch, returned to the fire, and sat down cross legged. He handed the pouch to Mime. "You may keep all the meat. And the pouch," he said.

"Thank you," Mime said. He took the pouch and hung it around his neck.

"Do you have much farther to travel?" the discarnate asked.

"We journey to Monglom's land," Mime said.

"A friend of yours?" the ghost asked.

Eeklan and Mime realized the discarnate refused to accept its death, and Monglom's hold on Langdom.

"No! No! Who is it?" the ghost shouted. "Leave me be! Leave me be!"

Mime and Eeklan were startled; afraid to move.

A grayish glow outlined the spirit's head. His features became more gaunt. His eyes turned black. "You have opened the doorway for me, Pourn!" a voice exclaimed, through the ghost.

Mime and Eeklan recognized the speaker.

Monglom!

The fire crackled unnaturally in its pit. Monglom was drawing energy from it. "You have gifted me your pawns and the weapon for their destruction!" he rejoiced, through the discarnate.

The hut began to breathe. The woven walls bent in

and out slowly. They sounded like four huge drums beating in sequence. Monglom was generating electricity with them, augmenting his power.

Monglom flowed his ire into the pit fire. It hued purple and several of the coals popped.

Eeklan started to draw his sword, but recognized the folly of it.

"You should not have hastened to the aid of a friend in the midst of war!" Monglom screamed, through the spirit. "You shall not *foil* me again!"

He caused the despairing ghost to coat himself with purple fire, then propelled him toward Eeklan.

The archer jumped up and aside.

Mime's legs refused to move.

Monglom spun the ghost toward the dwarf.

Pourn spoke through Mime with uncanny volume: "No! I came to *heal*! This must *not* happen!"

Pourn rendered the spirit motionless with invisible energy.

The walls continued to bend in and out. Monglom was still gathering power.

Pourn jerkily stood Mime up. "You must release my friend!" Pourn ordered, through Mime.

Pourn put more invisible energy into his hold on the ghost.

Monglom issued a howl, through the discarnate. The Wizard was straining to control the ghost. He was also struggling to connect with the electricity in the hut. He made the walls breathe faster; the drumming sounds became louder. The electricity generated almost crackled in the air. He caused the ghost's flames to reach out, like tentacles, toward Mime.

Pourn's words rose clearly above the drum cadence. "You must release my friend!" he stated, through Mime.

Pourn increased his energy hold on the discarnate.

The spirit's eyes turned gray. His flames changed from purple, to the crimson of fear and despair.

Monglom howled, through the spirit. He was straining even more to maintain his hold on the ghost. He managed a weak contact with the electricity he was generating with the walls. He flashed the ghost away from Mime, but at Eeklan.

Eeklan fell on his back to avoid the spirit's flames.

"By the rulers and powers of Afterlife," Pourn bellowed, through Mime, "release my friend! They so decree!"

Pourn grasped for control of the energy in the fire. The coals popped and the flames became red.

"No!" Monglom screamed, through the ghost.

The rage in his voice was almost a physical blow to Mime and Eeklan.

Monglom's ire enabled him to increase the breathing rate of the woven walls. The beating grew louder. The electricity this created turned the air blue. He sent this energy at the corpse and it jerked spasmodically on the mat. He hurled the spirit past Mime, forcing it to re-inhabit its body. The ghost's magical flames enveloped the corpse. Although they did not harm it, they were able to sear Mime and Eeklan.

"No!" Monglom screamed, through the ghost. "I deny the Afterlife's authority!" He seized control of the pit fire. It turned light purple, grew brighter, and crackled weirdly. He drew upon the energy in the flames.

"You are flawed!" Pourn shouted, through Mime. "You shall lose, because you defeated yourself, long ago!"

Monglom sailed the fire from the pit. He made it crawl in circles around the walls. This generated more energy. He pulled the corpse to its rotting feet and forced it to take one step forward.

The pit fire crept across the door, leaving a black trail of ashes.

Eeklan dodged around the flames. He ran to Mime and tried to pull him toward the door. "I will hack the way out with my sword!" he shouted. "Come on!"

Mime could not be moved. It was as if he were composed of metal.

The walls breathed faster. The flames on the corpse, and within the animated pit fire, became more purple. Their light, and the blueness of the electricity, bathed the interior of the hut.

Mime's and Eeklan's eyes stung from the illumination. The woven walls were buckling in and out faster than either man could follow. The drumming sounds shook the earth.

Monglom raised the corpse's partially decayed hand toward Mime's pale throat.

Eeklan deflected the arm with his sword and delivered a blow to the corpse's head, but the blade caused no damage.

Monglom's purple power flowed down the weapon and coated the archer, immobilizing him. The hilt was wrenched from his hand, and the sword flew across the hut, landing by the door.

The fiery corpse raised its hand toward Eeklan's neck.

Pourn's voice resounded throughout the woods: "*It will not be!*"

The full force of Pourn's energy blazed with pure white light. It over shone the purple radiance of Monglom's virulent might, slowly neutralizing Monglom's energy.

The ghost's fire flickered wildly, then sputtered out. The corpse fell to its back, its decaying eyes staring at the reed ceiling.

The movement of the walls ceased and their drumming sounds died.

The pit fire turned yellow with Pourn's energy and he settled it into the pit.

"*More powders!*" Monglom roared, through the

ghost. "*I must have more powders!*"

The spirit's eyes returned to their normal blue color, through Pourn's energy, but flashed black again.

"Renewed!" Monglom exulted, through the discarnate. "This war *will* be won! What? No! Powders—more—"

Monglom could no longer speak via the ghost. He clamped the discarnate's shining hands to the sides of his shimmering head and rocked him silently side to side. His desperation, deep frustration and rage contorted the spirit's features.

Pourn enveloped the ghost in a ray of blue-white energy, ripped him through the ceiling, and conveyed him into Afterlife.

Monglom screamed as though his flesh were being torn from him. His ire flared the pit fire into a roaring tower of flame, igniting the ceiling.

Pourn swept open the door of the hut.

Mime felt his muscles relax, and fled through the portal.

Eeklan snatched up his sword and raced after the dwarf.

The haunted hut became enveloped in flames.

Pourn covered it with a temporary magic dome.

The fire died and the tragic clearing was shrouded in darkness.

***

Mime and Eeklan fled through the woods. They

splashed across the last section of the spooky marsh, then struggled through the thick grassland.

A small woods appeared. They fell to the weeds and dried leaves beneath the WideLeaf Trees, and lay gasping for breath.

Mime still had the pouch the ghost had given him. They were hungry, but neither could bring himself to eat the salty, greasy meat. They just lay close together, waiting for their fear and tiredness to ebb.

***

Mime and Eeklan sat up. They leaned weakly against two WideLeaf Trees so they were facing one another.

Starlight illuminated their tired faces.

"I think we should put as much distance between us and the marsh as possible, before we sleep," Eeklan said.

"Are we not in the, Near Wastes, now?" Mime said. "*Is* there any, secure, campsite?"

"I know of one place that might be safe," Eeklan said. "It is a site Monglom probably will not expect us to be aware of, much less, enter."

They tramped from the woods into grass and shrubs. These gave away to extensive patches of weeds. An occasional woods loomed on either side.

***

The lonely full moon whitened the landscape.

The stone city Eeklan sought, gleamed like a dull gray pearl worn by age and weather.

There was no entrance in the first long wall, so they followed it to its eroded corner.

Halfway along the second wall, two tall iron gates glistened.

Mime and Eeklan paused.

The main street of broken red cobblestones was pierced by long stemmed gray flowers and led straight to the city square.

Mime and Eeklan preceded with caution.

The yard of the square was overgrown with weeds. More pathways of cracked crimson cobblestones, pierced by long-stemmed gray flowers, led into the various sections of the city.

The odor of must and decay was strong.

The center of the square featured a circle of six white granite statues depicting legendary warriors in full armor and carrying double edged swords. They were frozen in classic battle positions and stood on round bases of black stone.

Blin City was as deserted as history had recorded. It had been constructed by metal miners eighty years ago and had been abandoned twenty years later after the mines to the west had petered out.

When they passed through the circle of cold stone figures, Mime felt a chill. "The statues are coming to life!" he warned. "We had best retreat to the gates quickly!"

Eeklan turned around and struck the tip of his blade against the back of the helmet of one of the figures.

The chinking sound echoed around the square.

"See," Eeklan said. "Rock. There is nothing to worry about."

The statue raised its sword, spun around on its base, and knocked the archer's blade to the cobblestones!

Chapter 12

The Battle of Blin

Eeklan jumped back.

The rock warrior leaped from its pedestal.

"When will I learn to heed your hunches, Mime?" Eeklan said.

The statue lumbered forward.

Eeklan leaped away. He discarded his bow and re-covered his sword. "Get ready to run, Mime!" he shouted. "I will be glued to your back!" He parried a thrust of the statue's blade, then jabbed.

The statue ignored the threat and just missed slic-ing Eeklan's throat with the tip of its blade.

"Now is the time," Eeklan told himself. He ran backwards, with all due dispatch.

The statue advanced just as rapidly.

Eeklan threw his sword between the assailant's legs.

The warrior tripped and crashed to the cobble-stones, shattering into pieces.

"That is that," Eeklan said, "we can go on now—"

The soldier's rock hand and sword lifted into the

air. It drew back, then hurled itself at the archer.

Eeklan dodged left, raced forward, retrieved his sword, and spun around.

The disembodied stone hand swung its blade.

Eeklan ducked.

The hand and blade hummed past the archer's ear and smashed into the back of a second statue. The stone sword broke in half and it and the rock hand fell to the cobblestones.

The second statue came to life.

The third statue stirred and looked at Mime.

Then the forth, fifth and sixth statues raised their sharp swords.

The figures leaped heavily to the cobblestones. They advanced slowly, forming a wide semicircle.

Mime recovered Eeklan's bow and his heart throbbed.

The shattered statue was drawing itself swiftly together, piece by piece. Its hand and blade, beside the bases, skidded across the cobblestones, to link with it, and it rose, eerily, to its feet.

"*Pourn!*" Mime whispered. "We *need* you! Help us, *please!*"

Eeklan knelt on one knee.

Mime pulled an arrow from the huntsman's quiver, and nocked it.

Eeklan stood up, ready for battle. "Back to back!" he ordered.

Mime did not respond.

Eeklan glanced aside.

Mime aimed the arrow at the ankle of one of the advancing statues.

"Take the one behind," Eeklan said. "It will allow us running room."

Mime changed aim. He pulled the bow as hard as he could, and shot. The shaft careened off the statue's ankle without causing damage. "It is no use," he said. "I cannot put out the necessary force!"

"Trip him with it, then, and run," Eeklan said. "I will trail."

The closest statue swiped.

Eeklan ducked.

Mime ran toward the rear statue and flung the bow between its legs.

The figure stepped forward and the bow snapped, uselessly, in half.

Mime jumped back from the statue's sword, barely in time.

The rear statue advanced toward the dwarf.

There was a loud clang.

Eeklan's sword spun through the air, shining in the moonlight. It landed behind the rear statue and clattered across the cobblestones.

Mime threw himself on his stomach. He locked his arms around the rear statue's left leg and pulled back with all his might.

The statue swung its blade at the dwarf's hands.
Mime rolled away just in time.

The statue smashed its leg in half and toppled to the cobblestones, shattering to pieces again.

Eeklan dodged a third thrust of the statue nearest him, and turned around. He snatched Mime into his arms, leaped over the fallen statue, and ran.

Five statues lumbered in pursuit.

The sixth statue gathered its pieces together and swayed after its cohorts, but far behind.

Eeklan rounded a corner. He skidded to a stop and leaned against the bricks of a building. He held his breath, and listened, along with Mime.

The clicking of stone feet striking cobblestones was loud and clear. The statues were almost upon them!

Eeklan began to run. He passed along the building, then between it, and another.

The five statues turned the corner, where Eeklan had paused. They bore straight.

Eeklan seized this opportunity and raced back toward the city square.

Something white stepped from beside a house.

Eeklan shouldered into the chest of the sixth statue.

The figure fell to pieces.

Eeklan and Mime landed on top of the pile. They struggled to their feet, looking for the other statues.

"Make for the gates!" Eeklan ordered, as he swerved back.

Mime slid to a stop in the center of the square. He turned around and anxiously watched the darkness. He thought he saw something white moving toward his right, but he was not sure.

A figure ran out of the gloom.

It was Eeklan!

Mime let out a relieved breath.

Eeklan had gone back to recover his sword. It was bent and he was waving it as he approached. "That damn statue is together again," he huffed. "I saw it bee-lining toward the front gates. It will reach them before we can get there. Come on!"

They ran through the streets of the ghost city, afraid to pause for rest, knowing the other statues were somewhere behind.

***

Mime and Eeklan came up against the stone wall at the rear of the city.

Mime cursed. "No gates here," he said.

"That front gateway will be guarded by that statue," Eeklan said. He leaned against the wall. "The other statues will be scouring the city, soon."

"Can you jump and catch the top of the wall?" Mime said. The barrier looked impossibly high.

"No," Eeklan said. "It is at least twelve feet." He rubbed his beard with the palm of his hand as he thought. "But I *could* heave, *you,* up there," he suggested.

"Yes," Mime agreed, "but what about you?"

"Let us check some of these houses," Eeklan said. "Maybe we can find a rope, or some rags we can tie together. I can bend my sword blade, and make a scaling hook. You search over there, and I will go here."

Mime crept up the worn steps of his objective.

The old house was squat and simple; large enough to contain one room. The paint had been weathered away, and the tall door stood wide open inward.

The moonlight penetrated only inches through the doorway. The rest of the house was pitch dark.

Mime stepped into the blackness and stumbled into a broken chair. He paused, listening. He could hear Eeklan next door, cursing the dark. But he detected no threatening sounds.

Mime felt his way along the wall to his left, stumbling into other pieces of furniture. He paused again, but heard nothing, not even Eeklan's swearing.

Mime inched along the connecting wall, feeling for a window. There was a creak ahead and he stopped dead, holding his breath.

Eeklan said, "Oof!" next door, and the crash of some piece of toppling furniture followed.

Mime listened intently, but the creak did not come again. He dismissed it as the wind, or the settling of the old floorboards, and continued.

Mime congratulated himself softly. There was a window here. He unlatched the shutters and shoved them open wide. The comforting light of the moon whitewashed the room.

The statue stepped in front of the window, blocking out the light. An evil expression was frozen into its stone face. It raised its sword.

Mime cried out, and fell, face down, on the floor.

The sword struck the wooden sill, with a resounding thud. The statue yanked the blade free, splintering the sill, and slammed the shutters closed. It forced a piece of the lower sill into a space between the upper sill and the two shutters, jamming them tight. It turned, heavily, around and lumbered toward the door.

Mime heard the loud steps on the packed earth. He could only think to crawl into the darkest corner of the house.

The statue paused at the bottom of the stairs. It looked to its right, as if it had heard a noise. It faced the doorway and ponderously began to climb. The ancient steps sagged, squeaking frightfully, then one snapped to bits.

The statue's left foot struck the dirt under the stairs and the stone knee hit the top step. It lost its balance and fell through the doorway, onto its face. Its trapped leg ripped, backwards, through the lower steps.

Eeklan ran up the statue's back. "Mime!" he shouted. "Come fast! I have found a ladder!"

Mime scrambled to his feet, climbed over the statue, and ran out the door, with Eeklan.

The statue lifted itself to its feet. It kicked away the wreckage of the steps and followed after Mime and Eeklan.

Eeklan had propped the ladder against the city wall near the rear of the house which he had inspected.

Mime stumbled into the ladder and fell onto his back.

Eeklan dropped his bent sword, hoisted Mime onto his shoulders, and climbed the rickety ladder as quickly as he could.

The statue wielded its blade, shattering the bottom of the ladder to bits.

Mime pulled himself onto the top of the wall.

Eeklan caught hold of its edge, but his grip was poor.

Mime grabbed the archer's wrists. He pulled desperately, and Eeklan managed to improve his hold.

The statue leaped up, stretched out an arm, and grasped one of Eeklan's ankles.

Mime refused to release Eeklan's wrists, and followed the archer down.

The statue hit the ground hard, but managed to remain standing.

Eeklan's feet struck the statue in the chest. Mime's feet thudded into the statue's pale face.

The figure tottered off balance, then crashed to earth, splitting in half, lengthwise.

Eeklan, groggily, rolled off the statue. He helped Mime up, and they ran.

The figure swiftly pulled itself together and re-sumed the chase.

Eeklan led Mime, by a dizzying, circuitous route, back to the site of the shattered ladder. They could hear the statue running toward the square.

Mime leaned against the wall. "He is not very smart," he said. "I would have doubled back and caught us as we rounded that last corner."

"You would have run straight, just like the statue," Eeklan huffed. "You would not expect us to return to where we have no chance of escape." He drew a deep breath, and looked around.

The ladder was useless but the statue had fallen on Eeklan's sword blade and had flattened it.

Eeklan slipped the sword into its sheath.

Mime shrugged, and sat back against the wall.

"The moon will set soon," Eeklan said. He settled next to Mime. "It will be harder for them to see us. Maybe we can slip past the gate guard and escape."

"Perhaps," Mime said. "But remember, it will be more difficult for us to see, also."

Eeklan looked disapproving. "How about a little

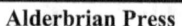
optimism?" he said.

"When it is justified," Mime said.

***

"Mime?"

"Yes?"

"Why do you suppose Pourn has not come to our aid against these statues?"

"I would guess he does not think we are really in danger."

"That *is* the way he has worked it, before," Eeklan said. "I guess this is what he will do now. Unless *we* can keep the situation from *becoming* desperate."

"I double hope so."

***

Mime's and Eeklan's elbows were touching, but they could not see each other.

"I believe it is dark enough," Mime whispered.

"Yes," Eeklan said. He adjusted his weapons belt so the sword and sheath were behind him. "Grip my sheath with both hands and do not let go, no matter what."

Mime did as instructed. "I will not lose you, in this spooky dark, by all that I find precious," he said.

They crept between the old houses they had searched, stopping every few paces to listen and to peer, hopefully, into the night.

They passed into the circle of black stone bases in

the center of the crumbling city square. Their skin was prickling, as it had in the hermit's hut.

"Monglom is gathering his energy," Mime whispered. "He is going to strike, soon. Where are you, Pourn?"

The Wizard formed his power into a, glowing, gray, net, above Eeklan and Mime, and pressed them, prone, to the cobblestones.

If he could have drawn his blade, Eeklan doubted the occult strands could be cut.

Monglom drew the energy out of the air. He swept a freezing wind around the tragic square, once, then kept it on Mime and Eeklan.

The six statues, bathed in the grayish light of Monglom's power, strode from the darkness, forming a tight circle around Mime and Eeklan. They halted only inches away, and lifted their stone swords, for the final stroke.

Mime and Eeklan watched, helplessly.

Pourn issued a command above the square: "*Do not kill!*"

The granite warriors swept their blades downward.

"*No!*" Pourn asserted. Above the netted men, he formed his anger into a blue dome of solid magic which intercepted the granite blades.

With flashes of intense red light, and loud popping sounds, the statues blasted into showers of coarse gray powder.

Pourn ripped open one end of Monglom's energy net. Mime and Eeklan scrambled through and raced toward the gates of the city.

Monglom angrily repaired the net and flung it after the desperate men.

Pourn intercepted the snare with his dome.

The glowing magical constructs collided and exploded with scintillating red lightning and tremendous thunder that shook the ground, neutralizing the power both conjurers had gathered for their hate-filled confrontation.

Mime and Eeklan charged through the gates and fled into the grassland.

Chapter 13

The Gulch of Illusions

Mime and Eeklan paused in a woods. Blue-white starlight filtered through the leaves of the tall Wide-Leaf Trees.

Mime sat down on the grass, with his back against one of the wide, black trunks.

Eeklan adjusted his weapons belt to its proper position, and joined the dwarf.

"I am not so certain we will survive, even with Pourn's protection," Mime said.

Eeklan looked at him, sideways. "Are you serious?" he said.

"No," Mime said. "But, I can not imagine a closer call than the one in the city."

"I do not even want to pretend to try," Eeklan said.

"Do you know what I would like, right now?" Mime said.

"What?" Eeklan said.

"Food!"

Eeklan laughed. "All right," he said. He stood up and headed toward the heart of the woods. He rubbed

his hands together. "I scent berries," he said, "and are they ripe!"

***

The woods thinned.

The star light grew brighter and bluer.

Eeklan stopped. "This is the wood's end," he said. "The berries calling us must live in that woods beyond this gulch."

The towering, v-shaped chunk of gray rock ran for several hundred feet. Its sloping walls reflected and intensified the starlight in an unnatural way, casting strange shadows among the boulders and rocks that littered its bottom.

When Mime and Eeklan entered the gulch, all that stone seemed to grasp at them with fingers of cold and it felt as if the sky was trying to crush them beneath its measureless weight.

Mime followed Eeklan around a boulder. He thrust his hands into his pants pockets. "Is this cold not peculiar for this season?" he said.

"Yes," Eeklan said. "This begins to smell of Monglom. We had best forsake our stomachs. We will double back and circle around this place."

"It is too late!" Mime warned. He pointed.

A line of tall forms stood on the summit of each rise. They were dressed in flowing black habits. Ebony hilted swords in black sheaths were belted around their waists. The air was dead still but their garments whipped and fluttered as though they were facing a storm.

Eeklan saw stars twinkling, feebly, through a few of the forms. "Illusions," he said, with relief.

"For how long?" Mime wondered. "Monglom will not stop at just scaring us. We had better run."

The figures drew their weapons, revealing transparent blades.

Eeklan and Mime were standing in the center of the gulch. Enormous boulders blocked their path in either direction.

Eeklan started climbing around the boulder toward the woods ahead. One of the spooky figures, on top of the left rise, swept eerily down to intercept him.

Eeklan ignored the threat.

"Your sword!" Mime warned. "The phantom looks solid now!"

Eeklan spun around. He pressed his back against the rough boulder, and parried the figure's thrust.

The phantom thrust again.

Eeklan feinted, then stabbed the figure in the chest.

The assailant exploded in an uncanny, silent, flash of gray light.

Eeklan returned to Mime. "Back to back!" he ordered.

"No good," Mime said. "I have no weapon."

"Use rocks," Eeklan said.

Moving in slow motion, the figures were halfway

down the rises. Sheltered from the direct shine of the stars, it was now impossible to see which phantoms Monglom had made solid and which he had left as illusions.

Mime hastily loaded his pockets with stones. "Lift me onto this boulder." he said. "I will tell you where the solid creatures are!"

Eeklan did this and turned back to the enemy.

One of the figures on the left rise swept forward.

Mime heaved a stone. "Only illusion!" he advised.

The phantom passed through Eeklan and into the boulder, from which it did not emerge.

Two of the figures on the right rise flashed at Eeklan.

Mime threw two rocks.

They bounced off the spectral assailants.

"Both real!" Mime warned.

Eeklan attacked, blocking the clear swords. He kicked one phantom in the stomach.

The figure toppled over, backwards, and exploded.

The second phantom advanced.

Eeklan dodged back, but the tip of the sparkling blade nicked his throat. He parried the next thrust, then ran the figure through. It flashed silently out of existence.

The phantoms began milling in eerie patterns.

"Eeklan!" Mime shouted, desperately. "I am out of stones! I cannot help you tell illusion from real!"

Eeklan attacked three of the figures. His blade passed through, and they vanished. Ten phantoms from the right rise started toward him. He retreated, tossed his sword to Mime, and scrambled to the top of the boulder.

"Pourn!" Mime shouted. "If we ever needed you, it is now! Pourn!"

The remaining figures surrounded the boulder. Monglom lighted them with a subdued, gray glow. The flesh on their faces was rotting. Their hands were human, but their fingers were like claws. Monglom withdrew the glow, and the grotesque phantoms began their assault.

Mime and Eeklan stood, back to back, in the center of the boulder. The transparent blades sliced the air, inches from their legs.

"Pourn!" Mime beseeched. "Pourn!"

One of the figures became airborne. Eeklan decapitated it, and it exploded in the eerie, silent, gray light.

Another creature rose into the air.

And another.

Mime whimpered. "We are lost!" he shouted. "Pourn is not coming! He is finally spent!"

Eeklan attacked the floating phantoms. His blade passed through them, and they vanished. "Mime," he said. "If I heave you onto that bolder, can you get down, and make it back, to the other woods?"

Mime almost sobbed. "No!" he said. "They are too

fast!"

Six figures levitated at the archer. Six blades nicked his arms and neck before he sent each phantom the way of the noiseless, light-burst death.

Six more figures soared up. Three thrust their blades at Mime. He cried out and grabbed his right forearm.

Eeklan blocked three swords simultaneously. The impact knocked him down, hard. He rolled into the dwarf, and Mime fell beside him.

The six phantoms swept their blades down.

Eeklan saved them, with an arm-wrenching, double-handed, blade-block, but his sword was dislodged from his grip.

Mime rolled reflexively away.

Eeklan kicked sideways. He booted the feet out from under one of the figures. It toppled into the path of the blades of the remaining five creatures, and all six exploded, in the soundless, gray light.

Mime scrambled to his feet, and froze.

The figures were gone, and the gulch was still. The silence was almost a physical presence.

Eeklan wearily stood up. He recovered and sheathed his sword. He inspected the cut on Mime's forearm and said, "It is not bad, just painful."

"I—I shall be all right," Mime said, exhausted. "What about you?"

Eeklan touched his numerous nicks and cuts. He

tore a strip from the tail of his shirt and tucked the shirt back into his slacks. He carefully cleaned Mime's wound, then he saw to his own. "We should be dead," he said, as he worked, "and I do not pretend to understand why we are not."

Mime wiped his brow. He noticed the cold was gone. "Monglom must have run short of his powders, or his endurance, and his energy must have waned," he said. "That could be why the figures were not solid enough to do much damage."

"Or," Eeklan said, "what we feared has happened; Pourn did not *arrive* to aid us. We might be on our own, *again*."

"Yes. Damn it!" Mime said. "But, perhaps Pourn pushed himself beyond *his* endurance, at Blin, and his absence might be temporary, as he recovers."

"It may not be," Eeklan cautioned. He threw the cleansing rag away. "We must proceed as if Pourn is no longer our protector."

Mime sat down, dangling his feet over the edge of the boulder. He looked up at the archer. "I do not like it," he said, softly, and shakily. "We need Pourn, more than ever. We are, too close, to Monglom, to lose Pourn, now."

Eeklan sat down. "We *can* succeed without Pourn," he said. "It will take longer. But, we *can* succeed."

Mime's face twisted with his despair. "No," he said. "Monglom leaves us nowhere to hide. He can sense our position, without the aid of his Riders. He will be able to see us over hundreds of miles soon and even through stone. If we cannot destroy him *now*, we *never* will. And without Pourn, or Armell's magic torches, it is *insane* to continue."

"But—"

"But," Mime interrupted, "it is *insane* for us to do *nothing*. The Evil One leaves us *no* option."

Eeklan closed his eyes and rubbed them gently. "It is even more so now: succeed or die. Kill or be killed."

"Yes," Mime agreed. "If Pourn can no longer help us, when Monglom strikes next, we *shall* die!"

Chapter 14

Like Ghosts Before Torchlight

A breeze swept a sweet scent out of the second woods.

Eeklan smiled. "Berries!" he exclaimed. "At least *they* were not an *evil* trick!" He slid off the boulder and helped Mime down.

"Eeklan?"

"Yes, my friend?"

"Do you really feel Pourn is gone? Deep down?"

Eeklan raised an eyebrow. "I—I do not know," he said. "I never, truly, felt he *was* here, though his voice and actions, told me so. Why? Do you sense him?" He looked, hopefully, at the dwarf.

Mime touched the cut on his forearm. "No," he said. His voice was sad, but his eyes were dry. "I do not sense him, either. I just do not know," he added.

They climbed around the boulder and entered the second woods. They picked and ate the delicious berries, in dejected silence.

***

"I do not feel like sleeping," Mime said. "I want to

move on, to hurry against Monglom."

"I know," Eeklan said. "We will reach the Blaine Spur of Mountains, soon. They are the original peaks. Monglom built his to the left and right of them. The Membling Pass is on the right of the Blaine Spur."

They exited the woods for the thinning grassland. The starlight was bright, the air cool. The Blaine Spur was a minacious black hulk to their left.

***

The wooded grassland made a gradual semicircle away from the brooding Wasteland.

Eeklan and Mime drew slowly nearer to the first peak. The sparse grass gave way to hard earth and scatters of rocks and boulders.

***

"Wait!" Eeklan warned.

Mime listened carefully but heard nothing.

They doubled back and crouched behind boulders. Soon, the sounds of hooves clopping on stone drifted around the rocks.

Mime was impressed by the archer's auditory acuity.

They peered around the boulders.

Two groups of mounted Riders approached each other on the side of the mountain. They had been hidden by outcroppings of rocks.

They did not wear habits and their gray body glows

spread an oblong of light around them.

The descending group had several pack horses loaded with crates of powder.

The ascending group had several pack horses loaded with parcels of food.

The skeletons reined to a halt and pressed their gloved hands to their foreheads in greeting.

"The Master will be pleased," the leader of the ascending group said. "His supplies of the powders grow low."

"The slaves are sluggish and lazy," the leader of the descending party said. "But we have tried new ways of speeding their work."

The six skeletons laughed, sounding like a harsh wind through a field of dried, rotting reeds.

"Hebon impatiently awaits those food supplies," the descending leader said. "He is determined to make the slaves work even harder to earn their rations. He wants to out-mine the other camps for the Life Boost Reward."

They laughed again and continued in opposite directions.

Eeklan watched until the noisy Riders were almost beyond sight. He prodded Mime and they followed the ascending party.

The path wound intricately up the side of the steep mountain, but the starlight allowed sufficient illumination for them to pick their path.

***

Eeklan and Mime followed the Slavers to a rock plateau. There was an old outpost on the left side. It was constructed of split logs and stood against the higher part of the peak.

Skeletons were stationed on the catwalks behind the walls. None of these guards wore habits.

The resupply Riders passed into the outpost and the gates were closed.

Mime and Eeklan took cover behind some rocks.

"What do you plan?" Mime asked.

"If we can free these people," Eeklan said, "the search for them will scatter Monglom's attention and his Riders. We will stand an even better chance of passing to Illkature even if Pourn *has* faded into Afterlife, as it seems."

"Must we endanger their lives?" Mime said.

"I do not like this any more than you do," Eeklan said. "But, if we fail to destroy Monglom, these people will never see freedom. They will suffer for the rest of their lives. Anyway, they will not be harmed. They are needed to mine. They will just be recaptured and replaced in the fortress. That will require perhaps, two days; enough time to see us to Illkature. We *must* have that time." He smiled, reassuringly. "Besides, I plan to *ask* their help. If they refuse, we shall leave them be."

Mime was relieved. "All right," he said, "I stand

with you, on that condition."

They crept through the boulders and rocks, toward the ancient outpost.

The Riders on the catwalks were armed with swords and bows. They were keeping watch of the perimeter of the fort.

The night, and the screen of rocks and boulders, plus the shadows cast around them by the stars, were sufficient to allow Mime and Eeklan to reach the front wall.

They slipped along this, to the left. There was a sheer drop at the corner. They leaped gingerly across this break in the plateau and stopped where the side wall joined the mountainside

Eeklan stepped back and looked up for sentries.

One Rider was posted halfway along the wall. It left its position and began speaking with one of the skeletons stationed on the catwalk of the front wall.

"How do we get up?" Mime asked.

Eeklan un-slung his quiver. "No problem," he said. He took hold of the bottom of the quiver with both hands and jumped up. He flicked his wrists and the loop of the shoulder strap landed around one of the pointed posts. He dangled about four feet off the ground. "Climb!" he grunted.

Mime frowned, but ascended, finding hand holds wherever he could. He stood astride the archer's shoulders, and froze.

"Hurry," Eeklan said. "I am losing my grip!"

"The side wall Rider is peering our way," Mime whispered. "It may have heard us."

Eeklan swore under his breath and tried to reaffirm his grip. The muscles of his hands were aching now. If he let go, Mime would tumble toward the break in the plateau, and he was not sure he could prevent the dwarf from plunging over to the sharp rocks below. His fingers began to go numb, and he could feel the quiver slipping from his hold.

Mime pulled himself over the wall.

Eeklan released the quiver. He hit the ground hard and dug his fingernails into the wall posts to avoid falling off the cliff. He massaged his hands until the feeling returned. He leaped up, took hold of the end of the quiver, and hauled himself onto the catwalk, beside Mime.

The Rider was again in discussion with its comrade on the walkway of the front wall, both looking toward the gates.

Eeklan left his quiver dangling from the post in the event of retreat. He pointed to a long, split-log building.

It stood just below them, but several inches from the wall.

They jumped to the roof and walked to the end which faced the black mountain. They swung themselves off the eave and dropped to the dark compound.

Mime and Eeklan peered around the corner of the building.

The blue starlight allowed them to see that there were no Riders at the entrance of the mine.

Eeklan led Mime along the end of the building and they peeked around its corner.

There were no windows in the structure, but there were two split-log doors. A glowing Rider guarded each.

Eeklan held his breath and pressed an ear to the side of the building. He touched Mime on the shoulder. "The slaves are in here," he said. "Some of them are talking."

"How do we enter?"

"Return to your post or Monglom will feed you to his weakest Yug Dogs," a voice ordered, with undisguised threat. The words came from the front of the building.

"I thought I heard a noise behind the prison, Hebon," a second voice said, defensively. "I was going to check."

"Very well," Hebon said. "*I* shall investigate. You remain at that damn door!"

Mime and Eeklan spun around and raced silently to the rear of the prison.

"Quickly!" Eeklan said.

He formed a stirrup with his hands, boosted Mime

onto the roof, hastily jumped, caught the eave, and pulled himself up.

Mime lay on his stomach beside Eeklan, almost without breathing.

Eeklan checked on the side walkway sentry. It was coming back to its position to retrieve its bow. If it joined Hebon's search, it was sure to see them.

Hebon rounded the corner of the prison. Though it was wearing its habit, the gray glow from its false face flesh and skull feebly illuminated the rear of the prison, a small section of the ground, and part of the wall of the outpost. It drew its sword and stalked to the far end of the prison. "There is nothing here!" it said, angrily. "You waste my time with your weak imagination! Do not allow it to happen again!" It sheathed its sword and returned to the front of the prison. "I will be in the mine for an hour," it said. Its tone indicated that disturbing its activities before that time had elapsed, would be an unwise act.

Mime watched Hebon enter the mine.

Eeklan checked on the side wall sentry.

The skeleton leaned its bow against the wall and went forward again. It began speaking with its front wall comrade.

Eeklan wondered what they had to talk of, then he returned his mind to their task. "We will enter the prison through the roof," he said.

"We had better make it hasty," Mime said. "That

jabbering Rider will sight us, yet!"

The roof was short sections of split logs nailed onto wide cross beams.

Mime ran his hands over some of these tiles. They all felt impossibly solid.

Eeklan drew his sword and shoved the tip between two of the tiles. He yanked down on the hilt and one of the tiles came free. He lifted four more before he had an opening large enough for him to fit through.

Mime sat down and swung his legs over the opening. He gathered the log tiles into his arms.

Eeklan laid down on his stomach, took the dwarf by the back of the collar, lowered him into the prison, and let him drop the last few feet. Eeklan checked on the Riders manning the catwalks, sheathed his sword, swung his legs around, then dropped through the opening.

It was almost pitch dark inside the prison.

Blue sparks jumped and a yellow light sprang up. An old man had used a flint and steel to ignite a stub of candle. His shirt and slacks were tattered.

A younger man held the candle. His clothes were just as ragged.

Eeklan motioned for the sixty men, women, and children to maintain their silence. He took the tiles from Mime and beckoned to one of the men. "I need your shoulders," he whispered. "We do not want to be discovered."

The man knelt on the wooden floor and Eeklan stood on his shoulders. He settled the tiles into place, but loosely. Any good wind would blow them away. He stepped down, took the man by an arm, and helped him to stand.

The slaves gathered around Mime and Eeklan.

"Now," Mime said, "we have come for your help."

"*Our* help!" the old man said, incredulously. "*You* are the only ones in a position to *help*!"

"Never mind that," the man who had served as Eeklan's step said, "what news have you? Is Pourn *really* dead? Does Monglom, *truly*, control *all* of Langdom?"

"Yes," Eeklan said. "That is why we need your help. We are fighting Monglom—"

"Then, an army *has* been gathered," the step-man said, excitedly.

"No," Eeklan said. "We are alone. But the soul of Good Pourn has been aiding us as much as possible. He has saved us from Monglom and his Riders several times."

"But, if you have Pourn's *aid*, why do you need *ours*?" the old man said. "We have no *weapons*. And we are outnumbered. They feed us only enough to keep us working, and we are almost *starved*. *You* must help *us*!"

"We intend to aid in your escape and that is how you shall assist us," Mime said.

"A *diversion!*" the step-man said, angrily. "We must risk *our* lives to save *yours!*"

"To *free* Langdom!" Eeklan said, sternly. "We believe we are the only men under any protection. We may be the *only* free men, and the *only* ones who *can* destroy Monglom. But, he has his Riders searching for us. He has located us before, with his magic, and nearly killed us. If he had to pick us out of sixty, or more, it would be more troublesome to divine us. He and his Riders would be far too busy chasing you, to hunt us, and we could more easily pass to Illkature."

"You *cannot* ask us to risk our *children,*" a woman said. She was beyond the light of the candle. "They have suffered *too* much, already. We did not bring them into the world to be *slain* by un-dead horrors!"

"Did you bring them into the world to *slave* to death?" Eeklan said.

"Besides," Mime said, "you will not be harmed. They will not risk losing your labor. You will only be —"

"You are *so* wrong," the old man said, somberly. "One of us was *murdered* just yesterday as an example. He gave his food ration to one of the ill children. They slew him for *that.* They would slaughter ten of us, for *escaping. We* cannot *risk* that. They would select some men, some women and *even* some of the children, and *kill* them. Can *you* be the cause of *that?*"

Mime shook his head, in shock. He stared at

Eeklan.

"Have you tried using the Evil One's powders?" Eeklan asked.

"I am a chemist," a man said. He stood just beyond the glow of the candle. "I have never before seen esters like his. I cannot identify them and I cannot ingest them because I do not know what proportions to utilize. To try trial and error would probably kill me, and I am needed here to treat sickness. There is no way to use Monglom's powders."

"We cannot leave our babies and wives to these monsters," the step-man said.

"Why did you come?" the old man said, bitterly. "It has only hurt us. Even our hope is now gone."

"We were not aware Monglom allowed his Riders to kill his powder miners," Mime said, softly. "We hoped they were instructed to spare all, as in the past. Monglom has become more malefic than I had imagined. I have misjudged him. I *am* sorry."

"Now," the step-man said, "leave the way you entered. If they discover we have *talked* to you they will *murder* one of us as an example."

"We would rather live in misery, than die in vain," the old man said. "If you *are* charmed by Pourn's spiritual protection, as you claim, we may yet be freed, *when* you destroy Monglom."

***

Hebon exited the mine and strode to the prison.

"What do you want?" he said, irately, to the door guards.

"They are talking again," one of the sentries said. "Those traitors said something about *escape*."

***

"Now, you have fated it!" the step-man said, furiously. "Now, they will catch you with us!" He looked terrified.

The old man blew out the candle and the prison became electric with apprehension. The silence was broken only by the coughing and sniffling of some of the slaves.

***

"Forget it," Hebon said, angrily. "The Master commands we make certain they live to serve him. All we can do, now, is lash them, when they disobey."

"Even if they attempt *escape*?" the same portal guard said, with intense irritation.

"Yes," Hebon said. "Our comrade who slew the slave yesterday was just blasted to powder by the Master in the heart of the mine. It required all of my wiles to talk Monglom out of destroying and replacing *all* of us. We will *never* maintain order this way!" It angrily stalked back into the mine.

***

Inside the prison, the fear that had built up since the slaves had been abducted was released, with a loud, collective sigh.

No more killings!

Blue sparks jumped and the candle was ignited.

Mime and Eeklan gazed around at the relieved faces.

"Now, what do you say, to abetting us?" Eeklan asked.

The old man chuckled. It was an uncertain sound. But his wrinkled face showed more strength. "We will dish them more trouble than a hurricane inflicts upon a dried leaf!" he vowed.

There were whispers of agreement from the men and women.

"All right," Eeklan said. "Let us get organized. We will soon have the blackest part of the night to assist us."

There were twenty men, twenty women and twenty children. The children ranged in age from six months to twelve years. They were all in ragged clothes, ripped on rocks in the mine.

Everyone, from the age of ten, to the old man, worked a twelve hour day. They either broke rocks or hauled heavy baskets of powder. Undernourishment and laborious work had wasted most of them to a near skeletal state. Many had colds, as the prison carried the chill of the night.

Mime was sickened by their condition but he could do nothing for them. He gently gathered to him the children who were not sleeping. He spun them stories of Langdom's earliest history. But he could tell they were too worried and nervous to be distracted and comforted.

***

"Mime," Eeklan said, "we are prepared."

Mime handed a baby to a twelve year old and joined the grownups.

There were men grouped near each door. Their only weapons were their fists, but they were eager to fight. The suffering they had endured had to be mediated in some way. Their pent up rage would be vented tonight, with a vengeance.

Five women had been delegated to guard the children. They would herd them toward freedom when the gates were breached.

The remaining fifteen women would be a second wave of distraction and attack. They, too, would use only their hate filled fists.

Eeklan glanced at the lead men.

They all nodded.

"Now," Eeklan ordered.

The slaves hurled themselves against the doors. The latches shattered and the guards were knocked to the ground.

Eeklan cursed. Torches had been placed along the walls of the fortress. The heartless, flickering yellow light illuminated the small compound well.

The portal sentries scrambled to their feet and drew their swords to protect themselves.

Eeklan chopped off the first Rider's head and stamped the skull to pieces. The skeleton's glowing brain squirted in various directions and its flesh, flat black eyes, muscles, ligaments, tendons and organs, faded away as its magic life dissipated.

Eeklan handed the skeleton's long sword to the step-man, then charged toward the gates.

Mime kept as close to the archer as possible.

The step-man angrily shattered the cranium of the second door watcher and followed after Mime and Eeklan.

The other male prisoners spread out.

The old man led half the irate miners toward the stable which stood beside the mine entrance.

The rest of the slaves headed toward a small, split-log barracks across the compound.

"Alarm! Hebon!" shouted one of the two Riders on the catwalk above the gates. "The prisoners are escaping! Hebon! Alarm!" It leaped off the walkway and faced Eeklan.

The second sentry landed in front of Mime. It sheathed its sword and grabbed at the dwarf, with both hands.

Mime ducked and rolled to one side.

The step-man decapitated the Rider, crushed its skull with his boot heel, and helped Mime up.

The first sentry swung its blade, trying to knock Eeklan's sword from his hands.

Eeklan parried the blow, executed a fast down stroke with the flat of his blade, and shattered the skeleton's skull. The brain exploded, in a silent flash of released magic, and the rest of the Rider fell to the ground.

The other catwalk guards leaped down and ran to face the archer.

The step-man led the skeletons away, assaulting them with his sword, and his anger.

The barracks door burst open and Riders charged forth. Three headed to the stable. The rest engaged the male prisoners in fisticuffs.

Several skeletons exited the old mine and fanned out toward the Rider barracks. This placed the male slaves in a pincer.

The enraged women charged from the dark prison and attacked the skeletons with fist blows.

The frustrated Riders knew they dare not use their blades. They began boxing with the women.

Two skeletons were shoved down and their skulls were crushed by angry feet.

The old man, and some of the other male prisoners, were leading horses out of the stable.

The Riders began fist-fighting with the slaves. The steeds spooked and ran back into the security of the stable.

There was chaos now, with the Slavers taking the worst of it.

Eeklan guarded Mime as the dwarf struggled to lift the great wooden beam that barred the aged gates.

Hebon charged from the mine, waving its sword. "With me!" it ordered. "With me! The two Monglom seeks death for are here! They lead this revolt! Kill *them*! *Forget* the slaves! Slay *these* two traitorous men!" It furiously attacked but it was no match for the archer's swords skill and muscular strength.

Eeklan chopped Hebon on the shoulder.

Hebon's arm and sword crashed to the ground. It retreated, waving its other arm. "*Here* I tell you!" it shouted, irately. "Kill *these* men! Monglom will sap away all of our lives if we *fail* to slay *these* two traitors!"

Eeklan advanced on Hebon and swung his sword.

Two Riders interrupted his blow with their blades, then thrust in unison.

Eeklan parried their strike, stepped back against the big gates, and bumped into the dwarf.

Mime fell to his knees and the great bar settled back into place.

The skeletons struck down at Mime.

Eeklan parried both swords. He dodged to one side, stepped over Mime, and led the Riders away from the gates.

Mime scrambled to his feet. He heaved, with impatience and anger at himself, and drew the beam sideways out of its brackets. He gritted his teeth, and shoved the gates open, about man wide.

The old man and the other male prisoners had crushed the skulls of the skeletons at the stable.

More Riders flooded out of the mine. They hastened to the stable and quickly gained control over the old man and his fellows.

The women had knocked several of the Slavers down and had killed them by kicking their skulls to bits. This had prevented the pincer against the remaining male prisoners fighting at the Rider barracks.

But the number of reinforcements pouring out of the mine was too great for anyone to overcome.

The women were forced to retreat into the prison.

"Where *are* all those Riders coming from?" Eeklan asked himself. He whacked the head off a skeleton and cracked a second Rider on a temple.

The skeleton went down to its knees but leaped to its feet again.

Mime turned to call the prisoners out through the gates, saw that there was no free passage, then shouted in despair, "*Pourn*, do not allow *this!*"

Eeklan split the Rider's skull down the center and turned fearfully. He saw Mime's stricken face and followed his stare.

A skeleton was standing in the mine entrance. In its trembling hands, was a Talk-Globe. Miniaturized and fully weaponed Rider after Rider issued from it. They floated to the ground, regained their true size, in an instant, and joined the fighting.

The battle was all but lost.

The women and children were trapped inside the prison. Skeletons were guarding the entrances from a safe distance. They took slugs at any movement in the doorways.

The male prisoners at the tiny stable were being held on the ground by skeletons.

The male slaves near the barracks were still fighting. But it was against ever increasing odds.

Eeklan raised his blade and started for the thick of the Riders.

"*Damn you!*" Hebon cursed. "I said, kill the two who Monglom *hates*! *Forget* the slaves!"

He was shouting in vain. His Riders were too occupied with the male prisoners to heed their glowering commander.

Eeklan sent Hebon's head flying. He stamped the skull apart. Then he took off the head of another Rider. Five more turned and attacked. He was forced backwards, toward the gates.

"Save *yourselves*!" the step-man shouted. He swept his blade down, shattering the skull of a Rider, distracting the other skeletons from Eeklan. "We will not be *harmed*!" he shouted. "*You can do no more!* Monglom sends too many of these horrors through

that accursed, magic ball!"

A slaver parried the sword out of the step-man's hand. An uppercut from another Rider knocked him to his back. Two more skeletons held him down by his arms and legs.

"*Eeklan!*" Mime shouted. "*We can offer no aid! Give it up! It is lost!*"

Eeklan cursed, spun around on one heel, and fled through the gates.

Mime led Eeklan across the small plateau, and down the path which led toward the base of the mountain.

Several Riders gave chase.

The litter of rocks and boulders, and the moonless night, served Mime and Eeklan well. They vanished from the sight of the Slavers, like misty ghosts before torchlight.

Chapter 15

The Magic Tunnel

Mime and Eeklan retreated into the grassland. They entered a woods and stopped in a small clearing. They knew Monglom would direct his Riders after them, but they were too exhausted to push on.

Mime dropped to his seat and fell flat on his back in the grass. He was already half asleep. "Pourn is gone," he mumbled. "Hope is gone. Life—life, perhaps, is gone, as well."

Eeklan only half listened. There was increasing cold emanating from The Wasteland. He knew it was a risk to build a fire, but the coldness was a far greater threat.

He searched around the trees and found two dried limbs and one thick stick. He took the strongest limb and bowed it loosely with a length of vine. He cut the other limb in half with his sword and sliced the halves along their lengths. He gathered some dried grass and leaves for tender. He piled them onto the flat side of one of the split sections of limb, until it was covered.

He sharpened the stick against the blade of his

sword and sheathed the weapon. He pressed the stick through the tender and against the limb beneath. He wound the bow string around the stick and pressed another flat section of the first limb to the top of the stick.

He drew the tree-limb bow back and forth swiftly. The stick squealed, smoke curled up, then sparks jumped. The tender ignited. He heaped more dried leaves, and some twigs on it.

He gathered fallen branches and placed them on the fire. They caught, and the campfire radiated an inviting yellow light, and a very comforting warmth. He rubbed his eyes, settled down beside the fire, and entered a deep, fatigued sleep.

Mime lay on the opposite side of the campfire.

They slumbered three perilous miles from the enchanted mountains and the gray domed, black blight known as Illkature.

***

Monglom sat forward on his throne. He concentrated with all his insane might. Yes! Yes! He could sense Pourn's soul nowhere on the planet! Afterlife had finally claimed damned Saint Pourn! That was why Pourn had not aided his pawns in the gulch and at the mining camp! He smiled grimly, leaned back, and closed his eyes. He was almost afraid to trust his discovery. But he finally allowed relief to wash over him.

He *had* triumphed!

Langdom *was* his!

Regretfully, it was still imperative that he destroy the ones whom Pourn had abetted. He could not leave them alive, should the inscrutable rules of Afterlife permit Pourn to return. Pourn would be able to wrest away control of both of those niggling puppets.

He began concentrating on Eeklan and Mime. He needed only to locate their general vicinity. Then...

***

Monglom sent his quiet, gloating laughter to the site where Mime and Eeklan lay. It was laughter formed in his deranged mind. It did not require breath and it did not cease.

An unearthly crackling filled the trees ringing the clearing. Monglom was drawing energy from them. They became enveloped in a dull gray glow.

Monglom coalesced that shine into a gray orb and floated it above the two men. He charged that orb with some of the power from his powders, and it burst into red flame.

Monglom lowered the fireball into the campfire and blended it into the flames. He ceased drawing energy from the trees and the ghastly crackling sound stopped. He squelched his mental laughter. It was time to strike!

Monglom called upon the powers of his powders. He bound Eeklan in a shimmering green case of energy.

Eeklan sat up abruptly and began shouting incoherently. He was utterly terrified.

Mime awoke, with a start. Fear stabbed his heart. "Eeklan!" he cried out. "Fight! He cannot control you, if you fight! Say your name! It is defensive power! Just say your name!"

Monglom deepened the green of the energy.

Eeklan ceased shouting. He began to fade from existence, like a dream faced with morning.

Mime hurled himself at the force enveloping the archer.

Monglom flared the emerald energy.

Mime stumbled backwards, stunned. He collapsed on the grass, and lay gasping for breath.

The soft glow of Pourn's energy coalesced in the tragic clearing. He made a replica of the dwarf's voice resound in Eeklan's Mind:

"Just say your name! Just say your name! Just say your name! Just say your name!"

Eeklan began shouting: "I am *Eeklan*! I am *Eeklan*! I am *Eeklan*! I am *Eeklan*!... " He became more solid inside the energy field.

Monglom howled through the fireball in the campfire. His voice shrilled with frustration.

Mime recovered his breath. He struggled slowly to his feet, snatched a burning branch out of the campfire and attacked the green power case. It exploded soundlessly and the light blinded him. The concussion knocked his breath away and flung him backwards to the grass. He landed just short of the campfire and lay gasping.

Eeklan continued shouting, affirming his identity and name.

Mime caught his breath and rubbed at his dry eyes. He struggled to his feet, and stumbled, toward the sound of Eeklan's voice.

Pourn placed Eeklan into a protective trance. The archer shuddered and began sobbing.

Pourn jerked Mime to a halt. He walked the dwarf to Eeklan and placed Mime's left hand on the archer's forehead. "You may cease now," Pourn said, through Mime. "You are now safe. It is ended. You will awaken and feel calm and strong again!" Pourn lifted Mime's hand. "Awaken!" he commanded. Then he released the dwarf's body.

Mime collapsed at Eeklan's feet.

Eeklan felt as though he had just emerged from a perfect sleep. He recalled all that had transpired, but without the fear, or any of the bodily pain. He calmly looked at Mime. Monglom invaded his mind with stark panic. He *must* awaken the dwarf! "*Mime!*" he shrieked. "*Wake up, Mime! You must wake up! Now, Mime! Now!*" Monglom caused him to slap Mime's face. "It is *not* too late!" he shouted. "It *cannot be* to late! *Wake up! Wake up!*" Monglom increased the sham panic. It became a snarling beast in Eeklan's be-deviled mind. "*Please* wake up!" he begged Mime. "*Please!*"

Monglom impelled Eeklan to lift the dwarf and to stumble toward the campfire. Monglom jerked Eeklan to a stop and forced the archer to dip Mime's head toward the hungry flames.

Eeklan resisted with all his might. "I *cannot!*" he moaned. His speech was being garbled by Monglom. "I *cannot! Wake up! Please*, Mime, *wake up* or we are *lost!*"

Monglom forced Eeklan to lower Mime's head closer to the fire.

"No!" Pourn warned via Mime. "Another *step*, and we *all* are lost!"

The Magician's light in the clearing brightened. Pourn floated Eeklan and Mime several feet away from the campfire.

Monglom stumbled Eeklan back to the flames.

Eeklan felt as though he were being tugged apart, joint by joint, by giant, invisible hands. He would soon faint from the pain, and the dwarf would tumble into the crackling campfire.

Mime regained consciousness. He began chanting loudly: "*Pourn! Pourn! Pourn! Pourn! Pourn! Pourn! Pourn!*"

The vibrations from Mime's voice supplied Pourn with added strength. He drew Eeklan and Mime a few

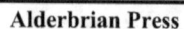

feet away from the campfire.

Monglom wailed in pain through his orb of magic in the campfire as he strained to draw energy from the orb and flames. He slowly slid the campfire toward Eeklan and Mime.

Eeklan was nearly unconscious but he still clung desperately to Mime.

Pourn's snowy white energy caused a powerful crackling in the clearing.

The campfire stopped crawling.

Monglom wailed through the orb in the campfire. He struck the WideLeaf Trees with severe cold. They were frozen instantly.

Pourn warmed Mime and Eeklan against the frigidness.

Monglom ululated more loudly.

Mime resumed chanting: "*Pourn! Pourn! Pourn! Pourn! Pourn! Pourn! Pourn!...* "

Eeklan was on the ragged edges of awareness.

Pourn instilled in the archer an understanding of what Mime was doing. He began bellowing with Mime:

"*Pourn! Pourn! Pourn! Pourn! Pourn! Pourn! Pourn!...* "

Pourn aptly harvested the power of the vibrations of their voices and deepened the glow of his energy throughout the clearing.

Monglom wailed through the orb in the campfire. He increased the terrible coldness with his hatred.

Pourn countered it with loving warmth. The trees thawed, and water vapor filled the clearing.

Monglom formed his fiery globe of magic and the flames of the campfire, into a towering, faceless humanoid, and directed it toward the hapless pawns.

Pourn extracted energy from the earth in the form of a mist and turned it into a solid white wall, between the flaming golem and Mime and Eeklan.

Monglom's effort to produce power made him ululate in agony. The trees around the clearing shook, as though in horror, at the ghastly sound.

Monglom enlarged the man of fire to three times its original height. He bent the golem over the magic wall and reached out its searing hands to snatch the men into its roaring, flaming body.

"*No!*" Pourn thundered. The lightning of his ire snapped all around the clearing. "*It shall not be!*" He formed the mist wall into a tunnel around Mime and Eeklan.

Mime was again unconscious.

Pourn swept away Eeklan's pain, and filled him with energy.

Eeklan clutched the dwarf closer to his chest and did the only thing a mortal man could when Wizards War. In panic, he fled down the white, glowing tunnel.

The conjurers slammed energy against energy in the aggrieved clearing. Scintillating lights flashed, visible even through the opaque walls of the tunnel, and

earthshaking explosions echoed throughout the land.

The magic battle was like an unimaginable lightening-filled tempest from the deepest chasms of hell.

***

The tunnel took a deep down slant, then it leveled off.

***

The sounds of the battle faded away.

Eeklan stopped running.

Pourn spoke through Mime's lips:

"*Flee!*" the Magician commanded, sternly. "*Flee!*"

Eeklan did not hesitate to heed their protector's words.

***

When Eeklan began to nod and falter, he realized Pourn was no longer supplying him with strength. He halted, and fell backward against a wall of the tunnel for support.

Pourn did not chide the archer through Mime's lips.

Eeklan sank to the floor of the trunnel and leaned back against the wall.

Mime's eyelids fluttered open. "It was Pourn," he said, tiredly. "He *is* with us, once again!"

"Yes. It *was* Pourn," Eeklan said, wearily. "We *are* safe, for now."

Mime did not hear; he had fallen asleep.

Eeklan nodded off, not realizing he still held the dwarf, protectively, in his fatigued arms.

Pourn began fading the tunnel; absorbing the energy.

Chapter 16

Illkature

Eeklan startled awake from a nightmare, jostling Mime to consciousness.

A yellow light from no source hung around them.

The magic tunnel had been replaced by one of blue-gray stone.

Thick dust lay everywhere.

They stood up and stretched.

Eeklan looked into the darkness on either side. "I suspect it is best to continue the way I was running in the magic tunnel," he said.

"If it is the incorrect direction, Pourn will probably let us know," Mime said. "He creates this glow around us, now."

"Where do you think we are?"

"Knowing Good Pourn," Mime said, "we are directly underneath Monglom's mountains."

"Too much to hope for," Eeklan said.

"If you were Pourn and your warriors were threatened with death, but they had only a short distance to go, where would you place them? If you could send

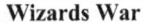

them anywhere in the area you might desire, except through the bubble over Illkature?"

"All right," Eeklan said. "I would put us right under Monglom's nose. But only if I could do so without Monglom detecting it."

"And, you would use the subterranean route because Monglom's bubble probably does not extend below Illkature," Mime added.

"Do you suppose Pourn has created this tunnel for us?"

"No," Mime said. "The dust shows its age. The walls must have been hewn by hand. Pourn's tunnel would be new and smooth. He would tend to perfection also, I think, making it more square."

They started in the direction in which Eeklan had been fleeing.

The light faded and darkness closed in.

Eeklan felt for Mime's arm.

They stopped and the shine misted into existence.

"I wish that light would not die out again, when we move on," Eeklan said. "I do not care to tumble into a mine shaft and break your neck."

"*My* neck?" Mime said. "How would *my* neck be broken in your plummet?"

"I would grab you and toss you to the bottom of the shaft so you would cushion my fall and then I would probably land on your neck with my head," Eeklan explained.

"Another of your father's tricks, I suppose?"

"No," Eeklan admitted. "My sweet mother banged that one into my head with a fire log one day. She intended for me to use my father as my safety cushion, if such a tragic occasion should arrive."

They resumed their trek.

The glow vanished.

"Since Pourn provides us with illumination just on rest stops," Mime said, "this tunnel must be safe."

Eeklan replied with a grunt.

Mime held Eeklan's sheath to keep pace with the rapidly striding archer.

Their footsteps echoed sharply in the shaft.

***

"I guess we are wandering in the correct direction," Eeklan said. "Pourn has not indicated otherwise. I still wish he would provide us with constant light."

They stopped and the glow coalesced around them.

"Why?" Mime said. "We have not bumped into anything yet. This tunnel seems to be a passageway—perhaps a quick escape route from the citadel—rather than an abandoned mining shaft. The only thing we are liable to blunder into, is the door at the end. We do not need the light."

Eeklan resumed walking. "When the grim drop comes," he said, over his shoulder, "I will make certain you precede me to the bottom."

The glow faded away.

***

"Eeklan?"

"Yes?"

They did not stop as they spoke.

"I understand now that Pourn *was* with us in the ghost gulch. Pourn was subtly sapping Monglom's energy. That is why some of the figures remained illusions and the rest were unable to really harm us. Pourn was slyly helping only enough to keep us alive."

"Pourn wanted Monglom to believe he was gone," Eeklan said, with happy realization, "so Monglom would not suspect Pourn's attack when we reached Ilkature."

"Pourn must have decided on his plan on the spur of the moment," Mime said. "That must have been at Blin City, near the end of his battle with Monglom. Pourn had to lay low suddenly. He could not even contact us through my mediumship. The energy required would have given the game away."

"When we went into the mining camp, we stupidly alerted Monglom to our position," Eeklan said. "We escaped without Pourn having to tender aid. But when Monglom struck us in the clearing Pourn was forced to defend us. We really spoiled Pourn's plan."

"Yes," Mime said, "but Pourn turned even our mistake, to his advantage. He fought Monglom in the clearing to keep him from seeing the route to the tunnel. Monglom probably does not have the slightest

inkling where we are. The Evil One is in for a real surprise when we pop up under his throne, or wherever
this tunnel leads."

***

Mime tugged on the sheath. "Let us pause for rest,"
he said.

"As you wish."

The friendly light reappeared.

They sat down against a wall.

"My stomach is asking if I have forgotten what food
is," Mime said, mournfully.

Eeklan took up the pouch that hung around Mime's
neck. He grimaced and withdrew a chunk of the greasy,
salty meat. He held it out to the dwarf. "Your banquet,
sir; eat and enjoy," he said.

Mime studied the meat with distaste. He handed it
back. "Thank you, kind and noble sir," he said. "I am
not *that* hungry."

Eeklan stuck the meat into the pouch. He closed
the mouth of the sack and left the pouch dangling
around Mime's neck. "Neither am I—yet," he said.

"Could your amazing father have fared any better
here?" Mime asked.

Eeklan chuckled. "He never mentioned caves or
tunnels," he said. "Biggest thing was a wormhole. He
swore they would yield food if you could manage—"
He abandoned the tale because his stomach, though
empty, felt queasy.

***

"Have you rested enough?" Eeklan asked.

"Yes. Eeklan? What will become of us when this is finished? If we are successful, that is."

"We will return to what we were doing before, I expect," Eeklan said.

"That will be very dull."

"I did not think you were unhappy being a teacher," Eeklan said.

"Neither did I, until all this happened," Mime said. "Now it seems as though I never was satisfied with instructing. Like I never fitted in at the schoolroom. Almost like I never was a teacher." His face was lined with confusion. "Ever since we found ourselves in this tunnel, something has been in the back of my mind. There is something I must remember or do not want to recall. But, perhaps I do not want to forget a moment of our adventure. No. I must remember something. Like a fact you fight to call forth to win a school contest," he said. "But it seems much more important than that."

Eeklan smiled with reassurance. "Every one seeks some grand adventure once in their life," he said. "You are just trying to remind yourself that you can not live like this forever. That no one can cede their security permanently. And that your true adventure *is* teaching snotty-nosed little rascals."

Mime laughed, then he looked doubtful. "Maybe,"

he said. "But I think not."

"You brood too much," Eeklan said. "That will make you old before your time."

Mime smiled. "I hope this helpful tunnel leads to a seldom used service entrance to Monglom's citadel," he said. "I would not like to come up in the middle of a Rider barracks."

"That is a horrible thought!" Eeklan scolded. "I would feel better if you had not said that! If it happens, I do not know you."

Mime chuckled.

They stood up and resumed walking.

The light dwindled away.

***

Mime pulled on the sheath.

They halted and the glow reappeared to comfort them.

"I wonder if Pourn is planning to execute Monglom," Mime said, "or to have us do it?"

"It does not matter *who* does it," Eeklan said, sadly. "Monglom *must* die because his drugs have warped him beyond saving. And, apparently, there is no prison that can contain him, surely, forever. To allow him to live, is unthinkable."

Mime tried to read his friend's expression. He could not. "I suppose we have no real choice," he said. "But, is it just and moral, to defeat one sin with another?"

Eeklan smiled sourly. "Either Monglom dies, or we do, and Langdom remains in slavery," he said. "We

must concern ourselves with what *is* not with what *should* be."

"You are not a stupid man, Eeklan. In fact, your knowledge and your reasoning astound me."

Eeklan shrugged and started off.

Mime followed.

The cheery light vanished.

***

Their footsteps were the only sounds.

Time stretched out so long it almost seemed to have stopped.

They had no idea how far they had traveled.

***

Pourn's yellow light appeared to their right, revealing a smaller tunnel which they entered. The rough hewn, blue-gray stone gave way to smooth, square, black blocks, and a solid ebony metal door stood in their path.

Eeklan tried the round black knob.

The portal was locked.

"I am sure we are about to enter Illkature," Mime said.

"We will know when I get this door open," Eeklan said. He struck his shoulder against it.

The hinges screeched, but the door did not yield.

Eeklan heaved harder against the portal.

The bolt on the other side snapped.

Eeklan pushed the door open wide.

Mime looked dubious. "Is it possible," he said, "those stairs could be an illusion, by Monglom, hiding that shaft, of which you spoke?"

Eeklan laughed. "If you are not careful," he said, "worry will get you before Monglom has another chance." But he tested the first step, with a cautious foot, before he placed his full weight on it. He drew his sword and held it ready, as though it were a charm to ward off evil.

Mime glanced down the dim stairway, to make certain no one was behind them, then returned his attention to their mounting path.

Pourn's yellow light came with them.

It was not a long stairway.

The landing confronted them with another solid ebony metal door.

Eeklan tried the knob and smiled in amazement.

The portal swung open.

The room revealed was enormous. It contained sealed boxes and broken crates. There was also much straw filler strewn about.

They crept between the stacks of boxes to the far side of the chamber and another black metal door.

Eeklan tried the round, ebony knob. He shook his head. There was no grille either, so he could not see where it led. He was reluctant to risk shouldering this door open.

Mime and Eeklan scuttled around in the yellow

light Pourn provided. They were searching for a pick lock, or other tool. When they split up, the glow parted and followed each man.

Mime waved something in the air. They met by the door and he showed Eeklan a pry bar. Someone had left it behind near one of the open crates.

Eeklan fitted the chisel tip into the slim crack between the door and the facing, and just above the knob. He pulled with all his strength. The outside catch popped up from its brackets.

Pourn's light faded away.

Eeklan placed the heavy pry bar on the floor and cracked the door open inward. Their storeroom was at the end of a hall illuminated by torches set in brackets along the black walls. The large, magical, ebony floor tiles showed no wear. A door, similar to theirs, was almost immediately to their left. It was closed. Halfway down the right side of the hall, a third portal was ajar and the room lighted. Another hallway intersected theirs. A door stood in its far wall. It was closed, hiding its secrets from them.

"What happens if they sight us?"

"We fight," Eeklan said, "and hope Pourn enacts his surprise for Monglom before Monglom deals his final blows to us." He pricked up his ears and pulled the portal to a mere crack. "I hear footsteps!" he cautioned.

Chapter 17

The Final Risk

There was only silence.

Mime wondered if Eeklan was mistaken.

The sounds of footsteps and of hushed male voices drifted down the hallway.

Eeklan and Mime peered through the crack between the ebony door and the facing.

"...truly is a twisted one," a first man said.

"Yes, rats eat his heart!" a second man replied. "But what can we do? We are under his power!"

"Who would have imagined this would happen?"

The speakers rounded the far corner of the intersecting hallway. They were the same size and build as Eeklan, and were dressed similarly to him. They walked, dejectedly, toward the hiding place, and paused in front of the portal.

"Which room is it in?" the second man asked. His shoulder was a hair's breadth from the door.

"The one around the corner," the first man said. "We had better make haste or one of his vile Riders will come seeking us. You know what that means!"

The second man shuddered. "Yes," he said, "and I do not even want to think about it! They say Monglom can be ingeniously cruel, when he is angered!"

They moved down the dead end hallway.

Eeklan eased the door almost shut. He was sweating. "Too close for joking," he said. He bent close to the dwarf. "Pourn has done everything, so far, but tie Monglom up and bear him to us. We are too near our goal to turn back, now."

Mime nodded firm agreement.

Eeklan opened the heavy portal. He looked down both passages.

Empty.

They stepped from the dark room.

Eeklan closed the door as noiselessly as possible and led the way to the ebony portal on the right side of the long hallway. He pushed the door open a little more.

A kitchen! It was lighted by torches set in brackets along the black walls. Ebony cabinets hung below them. Wooden tables, stools, and metal ovens, crowded the ebony floor. A doorway in the right wall led to an adjacent lighted room.

No one was in sight.

Tantalizing scents filled the air.

Mime and Eeklan painfully remembered they had not eaten in a long time. They were in the center of the kitchen before they realized what they were doing.

Eeklan roved his eyes over the dish and utensil cluttered tables. "Since we are here," he whispered, "we eat."

Mime did not try to voice objections.

They began searching the wall cabinets.

A man came through the doorway of the adjoining room. He was clad in white shirt and slacks and black boots. He bore down on the intruders. "What are you doing here?" he demanded.

Neither Mime nor Eeklan answered. Eeklan rested his palm on the hilt of his sword.

The man gaped at the weapon. Fear creased his face. "Only Riders bear arms here!" he cried out. "You must be enemy spies! Alarm!" he shouted, backing slowly away. "Alarm!"

Several men ran from the adjacent room. They were clothed like the first.

"These men are spies!" the first man said. "Let us take them to Lord Monglom before they cause us grief!"

An unusually tall man strode into the kitchen from the adjoining room. He wore a long blue robe.

"Armell!" Eeklan exclaimed.

The tall man gazed blankly at Mime and Eeklan. "I *am* Armell," he said, "but I do not know you."

"But you helped us just a few days ago," Eeklan protested. "You gave us your magic torches!"

"It is true that I once possessed two magic torches,"

Armell said. He was obviously searching his memory. "But I do not recall giving them away—to you—I do not remember you." He shook his head, mournfully. "I recall little. Monglom's Riders captured me at my home and brought me here." His sad face came alive with rage. "He sapped me of my meager magic like—like a Blood Snake sucks blood from a hare. Then he placed this invisible collar of energy around my throat and dispatched me to direct his kitchen slaves. I do not remember anything prior to my kidnapping." His rage turned into despair. "Nothing," he mumbled. He examined Mime's sympathetic face. "Why did I give my torches to you?" he asked. "Where are they?"

"You gifted us with them to enable us to reach Ilkature undetected," Mime said. "But Monglom located us by spell, or luck, or perhaps by reading your memories concerning our meeting, and sent a storm upon us. He destroyed the torches, and nearly killed us, which was his true intent."

"My magnificent creation, gone!" Armell lamented.

Eeklan turned to the kitchen help. "Why have none of you tried to slay Monglom?" he demanded. "Are you too cowardly to risk your lives?"

"We *have* tried," Armell said, resentfully. "But these abominable, magic collars will not allow us to succeed. If we advance to within twenty feet of him, the magic collar begins to choke us. It dims our sight, and we are

forced to retreat."

Armell's desperation spread to the other slaves. Their collective despair became almost tangible.

Mime and Eeklan were saddened.

"We cannot even poison what little food Monglom eats," Armell added. "The collar somehow senses it and punishes us. We can do *nothing* against Monglom!"

"But we can," Eeklan said, quickly.

"No," Armell said. "The second his sees you, you shall feel one of his damnable collars around your throat, choking the life out of you!"

"But, we have something you lack," Mime stated.

"Before we explain," Eeklan said, "We must have some food; we are half starved!"

"Of course," Armell said. He clapped once. "Some victuals for our friends," he instructed one of his companions.

The man went to one of the wall cabinets.

Armell sat down on a stool at the head of one of the long tables arranged around the room. "While we wait," he said, "perhaps you will tell us what aid you have against Monglom?"

Mime and Eeklan took the stools to Armell's right. Eeklan laid his sword on the table, keeping his muscular hand on the hilt.

Mime leaned forward. "If I were to tell you we are under Pourn's protection," he said, "would you believe me?"

Armell smiled, wryly. "Are you mad?" he said. "Everyone is aware that Pourn is dead. How can a deceased man, however powerful he was in life, be of any help?"

"Are you certain he *is* dead?" Mime asked.

Even Eeklan was surprised by the question.

Armell appeared doubtful. "Pourn must be," he said, "or Monglom would not have a stranglehold on Langdom, at this moment."

Mime shrugged. "Believe what you will," he said. "But, ask yourself how we came to be here. Monglom's Riders are everywhere. Could we have advanced this far, passed through Monglom's protective bubble, without some type of magical assistance?"

"What you say has the ring of truth to it," Armell said. "Pourn's soul could be aiding you. But, if that is so, why did he not prevent us from capturing you?"

"Are we captured?" Mime asked.

The man returned with the food. He set two dishes of meat pudding and two spoons before Mime and Eeklan.

They ate with pleasure.

Armell and the kitchen slaves watched impatiently until the intruders were nearly finished.

"I would have proof that Pourn's soul is aiding you," Armell said.

Eeklan swallowed a last mouthful of the pudding.

He snorted. "What would you have us do," he said, "summon Good Pourn here? Do you really imagine he would appear, just to settle a point for us?"

"We shall probably be strangled to death by these magical collars," Armell insisted. "We must have some sign, some small evidence, that Pourn is assisting you, that there is true possibility of success, if we are to join in. Is that *too* much to ask?"

His fellow slaves murmured in support.

Eeklan and Mime exchanged helpless glances. What could they do? Pourn came only when he judged intervention was warranted. Would he deem this one of those instances.

The kitchen slaves watched expectantly, awaiting a miracle.

Mime and Eeklan were not sure one would come. Time stole precious moments which could never be regained.

A soft light appeared around Eeklan's sword. It slipped free of his worn hand and stood on end, its hilt a few inches above the table top.

The kitchen slaves drew back in awe.

Armell sat where he was, watching with fascination. The blade tip lowered toward his throat. Blue energy flashed around his neck, casting weird shadows on the ebony walls. He raised his trembling hands to his throat. "It is *gone!*" he cried out, gratefully. "My collar is *vanquished!*"

The sword pointed to each of the kitchen slaves. Blue energy flashed around each magically encumbered neck.

"Pourn has freed you of your collars," Mime said, quietly.

The sword dropped flat on the table, without producing a sound, and the silver light subsided.

"Now, do you *believe*?" Eeklan asked.

"What do you demand of us?" Armell said. "Name it, and we shall give it our best effort. We must act quickly. It is morning, and the Riders are due within the half hour with more treasures and slaves for Monglom. This area will be overrun with them, and we shall stand no chance of success."

"Let hope guide us unerringly to our goal!" Eeklan exclaimed. He took up his sword. "First," he said, "where is Monglom, *now*?"

"In his throne room," Armell said. "He seldom leaves it."

"Show us the way," Eeklan said.

Armell led them to an ebony door in the far left corner of the kitchen. "We pass through here to take food up to him," he said. "He never descends." He pushed the heavy door open. A black stairway led up at a steep angle. "The portal you seek, is the biggest one on the landing."

"Send your men throughout the palace," Eeklan instructed. "Have them set up a clamor to distract

Monglom and his Riders. Mime and I will do the rest."

Armell waived.

The kitchen staff picked up pots and pans and any-thing else which they could use as potential weapons or noise makers and vanished into the ebony hallway like shadows before sunlight.

Armell warmly shook their hands. "Good luck to you," he said. "May Pourn's soul truly protect you!" He snatched up two pans and charged into the main hallway.

Eeklan and Mime looked at each other.

The time was a hand!

"I believe Pourn will neutralize Monglom's power at the strategic time," Mime said, "making the Evil One vulnerable."

Eeklan realized this meant he must be Monglom's executioner.

Memory whispered to Mime. A subtle change came over him.

Eeklan did not note this. He raised his sword and led the way up the stairs.

The landing was magically illuminated. A black door stood in the left wall. A larger portal loomed im-pressively at the end. This was the one they sought. They raced toward it; their hearts thudding in their throats.

The first door opened and a Rider stepped forth. It turned its hooded skull toward the footsteps that had

alerted it. When it sighted Eeklan's sword, it paused in surprise, then drew its blade and gave chase.

Eeklan heard the boots slapping the ebony floor and spun around.

The skeleton swept its blade down.

Eeklan jumped aside noiselessly, threw out a hand, and caught the Rider's wrist. He kicked its feet out from under it, and flung it onto its back.

The skeleton's skull struck the floor tiles and shattered. Its magical life force flashed briefly as it dissipated.

Eeklan yanked the Rider's sword from its gloved hand and laid it across its chest.

Several sets of booted feet slapped the floor tiles below the stairs.

Monglom was reacting to the noisy rebellion.

The Riders would be in the hallway, in mere moments.

"It is now, or never!" Mime urged. "Do not heed the other Slavers! They will perish when Monglom dies!"

Eeklan did not look at the dwarf. He expected the huge black portal to be locked, so he shouldered into it at full force. It swung soundlessly open. He stumbled, but regained his balance, and crossed the audience room, without slowing.

Monglom's pale eyelids eerily fluttered open. The Evil One stood up, in surprise. Rage reddened his

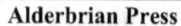
gaunt, skull-like face. Then supreme, mindless, fear distorted it.

Eeklan froze in his tracks. He followed Monglom's horrified stare, and dropped his sword.

Mime's hair had turned gray. His eyes were glowing with deep wisdom. He was very old. He pointed a forefinger at Eeklan's sword. It flashed through the air and cleaved into The Evil One's chest.

Monglom gasped with pain, utter frustration, and despair. He mumbled the one name he most feared, then slumped backwards, onto his ebony throne, and perished.

Chills traveled down Eeklan's spine. He turned squarely to the dwarf and smiled into Pourn's sad, but loving face.

Pourn had been forced to slay someone who had once been a close friend, and he was filled with grief and regret.

Eeklan nodded as though he had suspected the truth. "Finally," he said, approvingly, "everything on Langdom is correct. Everything is finally, perfectly, correct!" His thoughts turned, happily, to Windy, her friends, and the children.

The palace slaves began thronging excitedly into the throne room. They were already rejoicing the momentous victory.

Before they could see him, Pourn magically transported the stores of Monglom's powders to the monk's mines, sealed the shafts with great boulders, and vanished.

Without Monglom's enhanced psychic abilities and forces to maintain them, the Magic Mountains faded from existence and the protective bubble over Illkature vanished. The Riders in all areas of Langdom collapsed and lay still. The great palace shimmered and slowly evaporated, from the bottom up.

All that remained, was the stairway which led from the secret tunnel, and the household furnishings and sundries which lay in disarray.

Eeklan and the palace slaves were left standing on the barren earth of the Membling Pass, in the heart of the Harlan Wastes, near the pale body of their once mighty oppressor, and his grotesque, crumbling bodyguards.

Goose bumps covered Armell's skin as he felt his memories, knowledge, and psychic abilities return undamaged.

***

"The light around the door tells me we are well past the time the Riders should have ordered us to begin mining," the old man said. "There must be something very wrong!"

"I have heard no sound of the Slavers," the chemist said. "It is as if they have left the outpost."

"There is only one way to discover the truth," the step-man said. He shouldered the heavy door open,

shattering the wooden beam that barred it.

Sunlight lit the barracks and the slaves stared, with disbelief, at the discarded weapons, heaps of habits, and crumbling skeletons in the courtyard.

"They've done it!" the old man exclaimed, with joy. "Mime and Eeklan *have* defeated Monglom! The Evil One *is* dead, and we are *free!*"

"Some of you," the chemist said, "to the larder in the Rider barracks to gather food. The rest of us will prepare the horses for our journey home."

They cheered and eagerly set about their task.

***

The magical prison vanished, and Harkath, the Would be Wizard, awakened. The frigid winds of the Harlan Wastes fluttered his habit, but the bright morning sun warmed him. He glanced over his shoulder. Monglom's one hundred Riders lay in a heap of rotting habits and powdered bones.

A brilliant white light filled with love and compassion appeared.

Though anguished by the harm he knew he must have caused by his accidental release of the Evil One, Harkath's heart raced with relief and joy. Before the Would be Wizard stood Pourn.

"We work well together," Pourn said, softly.

The words astounded Harkath.

"I shall restore your psychic abilities and memories, which I hid behind those I spun for Monglom."

Harkath was inundated with recollections of long meetings with Pourn and Pourn's instilling within him the psychic energies he utilized to free Monglom. "Please, sir," he said, quickly, "do not return control of psychic forces to me. I am as flawed as was Monglom. I deceived you as to my true intent. I would have battled with you for supremacy had I succeeded in gaining the secrets of Monglom's powders. Few there are who can wield magical powers such as yours without succumbing to their own inner imperfections."

"All of these matters were known to me when I selected you as my ally against poor Monglom," Pourn said.

"I no longer seek to decree rules. I need to find my family. To make whatever amends are possible for any harm we may have caused them by releasing Monglom. To assist them to have happier lives. And to be at peace," Harkath vowed.

"Fear not, your loved ones eagerly await you," Pourn said. "Walk with me. It is well that you have faced your faults and limitations and realized the true joys of life, for you and I and Eeklan still have much to do."

www.ingramcontent.com/pod-product-compliance
Lightning Source LLC
Chambersburg PA
CBHW071153260626
47162CB00003B/1026